哈福

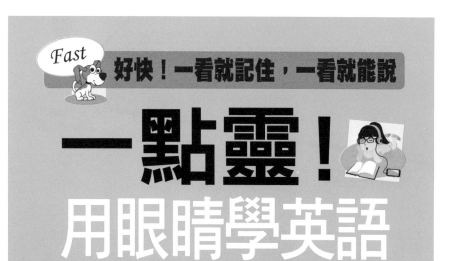

Fast

好快！一看就記住，一看就能說

一點靈！
用眼睛學英語

附 MP3

張瑪麗◎著

哈福

我的第一本會話學習書

速說學英語

你還記得你怎麼學中文的嗎？沒錯，就是用看的，從看圖文書開始。在你會看中文之前，在你會寫中文之前，在你還很小的時候，你周遭的人在講話，你就跟著說，你絕不會在乎你說的對不對，好像你每講一個字，一句話，身旁的大人都覺得很不可思議，你就越講越高興，我們就用同樣的方法來學英語吧。

我們美國公司所製作的每一本英語學習書，都是模擬美國人每天說的話，你在我們所製作的英語書裡，所學到每一句英語，都可以隨時用來跟美國人說，美國人一定聽得懂，每一句話保證都是純美語，我們要你天天聽，時時聽，有空就聽，聽了之後，你就得跟著說，那如果聽不懂，怎麼跟著說呢？

所以，我們錄製 MP3 時，都會有先用慢慢的速度念，我們要求美籍老師慢慢唸的原因就是，要讓你先聽得懂，這樣你才能夠跟著說。

速聽學英語

你看電視或是看電影的時候，會不會覺得美國人說英語說的很快，好像每一個字都是連成一個字說出來的，實際上，美國人還是一字一字分開說的，只是語調的關係，所以聽起來，好像一句話裡的每個字都是連成一個字。

　　我們的 MP3 先以慢的速度念給你聽，目的在讓你聽得懂，可以跟著唸，等你會跟著唸之後，你還要學會聽懂美國人說英語的正常語調，你如果能夠聽熟他們的語調，你會發現，他們說的英語其實也是一個字一個字的說的。當你聽得懂，又能和美國老師一樣速度說英語時，你就是從騎著三輪車慢吞吞學英語的階段，進步到開著快速的法拉利跑車飛速學英語的階段了。

　　每一個學習英語的人最大的希望是什麼？那就是能以英語適切流利的表達自己的意見，用英語與人溝通、與人洽談生意。我在此預祝你學英語的路程突飛猛進。

English　SAY　&　DO
這是人們的記憶
讀來的，記得 10　%
聽來的，記得 20　%
看來的，記得 30　%
看又聽的，記得一半
說出口的，記得 70%
說了並做的，記得 90　%

　　所以，你在學英語的時候，聽了之後，要記得說出口噢！

Contents

Contents

Chapter 1

暢談選舉

Unit

MP3-2

All of the candidates are real strong.
（所有候選人都很有實力。）

談市長選舉

A What do you think about the mayoral race?
（這次市長選舉你的看法如何？）

B Whoever is elected, the city will be better off.
（不管誰選上，本市都會更好。）

All of the candidates are real strong.
（所有候選人的實力都很強。）

A We do have a good selection this time.
（我們這一次真的可以好好選擇一下。）

Maybe this city will finally be able to solve the problems.
（或許本市終於可以解決所有的問題了。）

B I don't know about that.
（那我倒是不敢說。）

The mayor is only one of the officials.
（市長只不過是官員裏的一位。）

The City Council will have to change how it does things, too.

（市議會也得改變它的作風。）

A That's true.

（說的也是。）

句型靈活應用

· **表示會更好，怎麼說？**

The city will be better off.

（本市會變得更好。）

· **對別人的說法表示存疑，怎麼說？**

I don't know about that.

（那我倒是不敢說。）

文法句型練習

> whoever ＋動詞＋另一個句子
> （不管誰～，都會～）

＊ whoever 在這裡當主詞用，表示「不管是誰」。

▶ Whoever is elected, the city will be better off.
（不管誰選上，本市都會變得更好。）

▶ Whoever told you that, it's not true.
（不管是誰跟你說的，那都不是事實。）

selection	[sə'lɛkʃən]	選擇
mayoral	['meɚəl]	市長的
race	[res]	競賽
candidate	['kændədet]	候選人
mayor	['meɚ]	市長
official	[ə'fɪʃəl]	官員
council	['kaʊnsəl]	議會

| better off | | 會更好 |

Unit

MP3-3

Please vote for me.

（敬請惠賜一票。）

談選舉的意義

A Are you planning on voting in the city?
elections?

（這次本市的選舉你打算投票嗎？）

B I don't know yet.

（我還不曉得。）

Sometimes I really question whether it makes
a difference.

（有時候我真懷疑投不投票有什麼不同。）

A I know what you mean.

（我知道你的意思。）

But I have to keep voting.

（不過我還是得去投票。）

Free elections are part of the basis of our
society.

（自由選舉是我們社會基礎的一部分。）

B Yes, but are they really free?

（話雖是這樣說，但真的是自由選舉嗎？）

Could I vote for you if I wanted?

（如果我想選你，就可以選你嗎？）

A Well, not exactly.

（噢，那也不盡然。）

B Not at all.

（根本不行。）

You have to get on the ballot first.

（首先，你必須要登記在選票上。）

That's not exactly a free election, is it?

（所以，那就談不上真正的自由選舉了，對嗎？）

句型靈活應用

・ **問別人是否計劃要做某事，怎麼說？**

Are you planning on voting in the city elections?

（這次本市選舉你打算投票嗎？）

Are you planning on running for mayor?

（你打算競選市長嗎？）

・ **得到提名，名字上了選票，怎麼說？**

You have to get on the ballot first.

（你必須先受到提名，登記在選票上。）

Did you get on the ballot?

（你有沒有得到提名？）

> That's not ～ , is it?
> （那不是～，是不是？）

＊ 本句型是附加問句的用法，因為句子前部分是否定式 That's not，所以附加問句要用肯定 is it?。

▶ **That's not exactly a free election, is it?**
（那並不是真正的自由選舉，是不是？）

▶ **That's not exactly a praise, is it?**
（那並不是真正的誇讚，對不對？）

談天必用單字

vote	[vot]	投票
election	[ɪ'lɛkʃən]	選舉
society	[sə'saɪətɪ]	社會
ballot	['bælət]	選票
praise	[prez]	誇讚

談天必用片語

plan on		計劃做～

Unit

MP3-4

Who are you going to vote for?
（你打算選誰？）

談選舉並提及對政客的不滿

A Who are you going to vote for in this year's elections?
（今年選舉你打算選誰？）

B Any one who is not an incumbent will do.
（只要不是競選連任的任何一人都可以。）

A Why this anti-incumbency?
（你為什麼反對競選連任呢？）

B Very simple.
（很簡單。）
I'm tired of professional politicians.
（我對職業政客已經厭倦。）

A I understand your frustration.
（我知道你的挫折感。）
But some of them are okay.
（不過有些競選連任的也還好。）

B Only because they haven't been there long enough.
（那是因為他們在位還不夠久。）

句型靈活應用

- **口語上可以用 who，而不用 whom 做動詞的受詞**

  Who are you going to vote for in this year's elections?
  （今年選舉你打算選誰？）

  Who are you going to invite to the party?
  （你宴會打算邀請誰？）

文法句型練習

> Any one＋關係子句＋ will do.
>
> （任何～的一個人都可以）

＊ who 當關係代名詞，所帶出的關係子句用來說明 any one，表示任何一位由「關係子句」所界定的人都可以。

▶ Any one who is not an incumbent will do.
（只要不是競選連任的任何一人都可以。）

▶ Any one who can speak English will do.
（只要會説英語的任何一人都可以。）

談天必用單字

frustration	[frʌsˈtreʃən]	挫折感
incumbent	[ɪnˈkʌmbənt]	連任
anti	[ˈæntɪ]	反對
professional	[prəˈfɛʃənḷ]	職業的
politician	[ˌpɑləˈtɪʃən]	政客

談天必用片語

be tired of	感到厭倦

Unit

MP3-5

I'm going to work on Mr. Lin's campaign.
（我要為林先生助選。）

談助選

Ⓐ Are you going to work on anyone's campaign this year?
（你今年要不要幫誰助選呢？）

Ⓑ I don't think so.
（我想不會。）
I really don't have the time to devote to it.
（我實在沒有時間可以投入。）

Ⓐ I'm not going to, either.
（我也不會去助選。）

Ⓑ You are not working.
（你沒有在工作。）
I thought you may like to have a part in it.
（我原以為你可能會參與一份的。）

Ⓐ Not this time.
（這次不會。）
I need to take a break.
（我必須休息一次。）

句型靈活應用

· **替人助選，怎麼說？**

Are you going to work on anyone's campaign this year?
（你今年要不要幫任何人助選呢？）

I'm not going to work on anyone's campaign this year.
（今年我不會幫任何人助選。）

I'm going to work on Mr. Lee's campaign.
（我要幫李先生助選。）

· **沒有上班，怎麼說？**

You are not working.　（你沒有上班。）

Are you working?　（你有上班嗎？）

I'm not working.　（我沒有上班。）

文法句型練習

> I thought you may ～
> （我原以為你可能會～）

＊ 猜測別人可能會做某事，「以為」(think)這個字用過去式 (thought)，表示「原本以為」的意思。

▶ I thought you may like to have a part in it.
（我原本以為你可能會參與一份。）

▶ I thought you may like the movie.
（我原本以為你可能會喜歡這部電影。）

▶ I thought you may not have any interest in it.
（我原本以為你可能沒有興趣。）

> 主詞＋否定的動詞 , ＋ either.
> （也不～）

＊ 對方表示不會做某事，或不會怎樣；答者表示他「也不會」，
要用否定句再加 either。

▶ I'm not going to, either.
（我也不會。）

▶ I'm not sure about it, either.
（我也不太確定。）

> I don't have the time ＋不定詞
> （我沒有時間做～）

＊ I don't have the time 後面所接的不定詞 to，就是我沒有時間去
做的「那件事」。

▶ I don't have the time to devote to it.
（我沒有時間投入。）

▶ I don't have the time to practice.
（我沒有時間練習。）

談天必用單字

campaign	[kæm′pen]	競選
devote	[dɪ′vot]	投入

談天必用片語

devote to	全力投入
have a part in	參與一份

20

Unit

MP3-6

It is time for the presidential election.
（又是選舉總統的時候了。）

談總統選舉

A I can't believe it is time again for the presidential election.
（我真不敢相信又是選舉總統的時候了。）

B I hear you.
（你說得對。）

This time is different though.
（但是這一次不同。）

It's the first time we are able to vote for the president.
（這是第一次我們可以選總統。）

A I like to vote for the candidate that I think is the best.
（我要選我認為最好的候選人。）

But I hope the whole campaigning will be peaceful.
（但是我希望整個競選活動會是和平的。）

B I hope so, too.

（我也這樣希望。）

Who are you voting for?
（你要投票給誰？）

A I don't know yet.

（我還不知道。）

Have you decided who to vote for?
（你決定要投票給誰了嗎？）

B I think I have.

（我想我已經決定了。）

But I won't tell anyone until I vote.
（但是投票前我不會告訴任何人。）

句型靈活應用

• **表示對某事不可置信，怎麼說？**

I can't believe it is time again for the presidential election.

（我真不敢相信又是選舉總統的時候了。）

I can't believe that it is time again for the New Year.

（我真不敢相信又要過新年了。）

• **表示了解對方所說的，怎麼說？**

I hear you.

（你說得對。）

You are right.

（你說得對。）

文法句型練習

> not ～ until ～
>
> （到某個時候才會～）

＊ not until 表示不到某個時候不會怎樣，也可以說是到某個時候才會怎樣。

▶ **I won't tell anyone until I vote.**

（投票之前我不會說的。）

▶ **He won't be back until three o'clock.**

（他 3 點才會回來。）

Have you decided ＋疑問詞＋不定詞？

＊ "who, what, where, how" 等疑問詞加不定詞做 decide 的受詞，表示要決定的「人、事、地和方法」。

▶ **Have you decided who to vote for?**

（你決定要投票給誰了嗎？）

▶ **Have you decided what to buy?**

（你決定要買什麼了嗎？）

談天必用單字

| presidential | [prɛzɪˈdɛnʃəl] | 總統的 |

election	[ɪˈlɛkʃən]	選舉
believe	[bɪˈliv]	相信
different	[ˈdɪfərənt]	不同的
though	[ðo]	但是
campaigning	[kæmˈpenɪŋ]	競選活動
candidate	[ˈkændədet]	候選人

談天必用片語

vote for	投票贊成
vote against	投票反對

Chapter 2

美語晴雨計

Unit

MP3-7

It sure is hot and muggy today.
（今天真的又熱又悶。）

見面時，寒暄談論天氣

A It sure is hot and muggy today.
（今天又熱又悶。）

B Yes, but it looks like it might rain.
（是呀，看起來像要下雨的樣子。）

A Do you think so?
（你這樣認為嗎？）
It doesn't really look like it to me.
（我看是不會吧。）

B Well, this time of year you never know.
（噢，每年的這個時候很難說。）

A That's true and some rain certainly would cool things off.
（這是實話，下點雨的確會涼爽一點。）

B You're right.

（你説得對。）

I do think it will rain.
（我真的認為會下雨。）

句型靈活應用

· **天氣很熱或很冷，怎麼說？**

It sure is hot and muggy today.
（今天又熱又悶。）

It sure is cold and windy today.
（今天又冷，風又大。）

· **有人提了一些看法，你不甚同意，怎麼說？**

A It looks like the economy is turning around.
（看起來經濟有點轉機。）

B It doesn't really look like it to me.
（我看可不是這樣。）

文法句型練習

> I do think it will rain.
> （我的確認為會下雨。）

* 在動詞前面加上 do 是加強語氣的說法，強調這個動詞。

▶ I do hope he will come.
（我真的希望他會來。）

▶ I do believe the interest rate will go down.
（我真的相信利率會降低。）

> It looks like ＋子句
> （看起來好像～）

* It looks like 是一句常用的起頭語，表示「好像」，帶出後面整個句意。所以 It looks like 後面要接子句。

▶ It looks like it might snow.
（看起來可能會下雪。）

▶ It looks like we are going to have a white Christmas.
（看起來我們會有一個銀色的聖誕節。）

▶ It looks like the economy is turning around.
（看起來經濟是有轉機。）

談天必用單字

certainly	[ˈsɝtənlɪ]	當然地
economy	[ɪˈkɑnəmɪ]	經濟
muggy	[ˈmʌgɪ]	悶熱的

談天必用片語

look like	看起來好像
cool things off	一切都涼爽下來
turn around	事情有轉機
white Christmas	銀色聖誕（指有下雪的聖誕節）

Unit

MP3-8

We had golf-ball-size hail.
（我們這裏下了像高爾夫球大小的冰雹。）

兩人在談論前一晚下的冰雹

A What did you think about those thunderstorms last night?
（你覺得昨天晚上的大雷雨怎麼樣？）

B It was pretty bad.
（下得真大。）
We had golf-ball-size hail.
（我們那兒下了像高爾夫球大小的冰雹。）

A Wow! Did you get your car in the garage?
（哇，你有沒有把車子開進車庫？）

B Yes.
（有。）

A That's good.
（那還好。）
It looks like we got by without any major damage.
（看來這次我們逃過了，沒有什麼大損失。）

B Yes, just a really good light and sound show.
（是啊，只不過欣賞了一場精采的聲光表演。）

· 有人問你某件事的情況，你怎麼回答？

It was pretty bad.
（那真的很糟糕。）

It was good.
（那很好。）

· 有人告訴你一件好消息時，你怎麼回答？

That's good.
（那很好。）

That's great.
（那太好了。）

文法句型練習

What did you think about ＋名詞？
（你認為～怎麼樣？）

＊ 問對方對過去某件事的看法如何，要用 "What did you ～ ?"

▶ What did you think about the baseball game last night?
（你覺得昨天晚上的棒球賽如何？）

▶ What did you think about those thunderstorms last night?
（你覺得昨天晚上的大雷雨如何？）

What do you think about ＋名詞？
（你認為～怎麼樣？）

* 問你現在對某事的看法如何，要用 "What do you ～ ?"

▶ What do you think about the color?
（你覺得顏色如何？）

▶ What do you think about the suit?
（你覺得這件套裝如何？）

> We got by without ＋名詞.
> （我們沒有～而度過。）

* without 是介系詞，後面要接名詞，如果後面接的是動詞，要把該動詞改成「動名詞」。例如以下例句中的 speaking。

▶ We got by without any hurt.
（我們逃過了，沒有受傷。）

▶ We passed by each other without speaking.
（我們擦身而過彼此都沒有說話。）

談天必用單字

golf ball	[ˈgɑlf bɔl]	高爾夫球
hail	[hel]	冰雹
garage	[gəˈrɑʒ]	車庫
major	[ˈmedʒɚ]	重大的
damage	[ˈdæmɪdʒ]	損害
thunderstorm	[ˈθʌndɚˌstɔrm]	雷雨交加

談天必用片語

think about		想著
get by		經過；度過

Unit

MP3-9

It might snow tonight.
（今晚可能會下雪。）

Ⓐ The weatherman said it might snow tonight.
（氣象預報員說今晚可能會下雪。）

Ⓑ Well, it is cold enough to snow.
（真的，要下雪的話，今天夠冷了。）

Ⓐ That's fine with me, as long as it is just snow and not ice.
（對我來講沒有問題，只要下的是雪而不是冰。）

Ⓑ Really, if it ices I won't leave the house.
（真的，要是下冰的話，我就不離開家。）

Ⓐ Neither will I.
（我也不會。）

句型靈活應用

・ 如何說某一件事是可能的

It might snow.
（可能會下雪。）

He might be sick.
（他可能生病了。）

- **對別人的提議，如何表示你不介意？**

  🄰 I'm using your computer, if you don't use it.
  （你要是不用你的電腦的話，我就要用。）

  🄱 That's fine with me.
  （我這邊沒有問題。）

- **用 really 來回答，表示你真的很同意**

  🄰 The economy is bad enough.
  （經濟真的很糟。）

  🄱 Really, the unemployment rate is rising rapidly.
  （真的，失業率正急遽上升。）

文法句型練習

> It is ＋形容詞＋ enough to ＋動詞.
> （夠～所以會～。）

＊ "enough" 要放在形容詞的後面。

▶ It was cold enough to make water frozen.
（今天冷得可以讓水結冰。）

▶ I'm old enough to take care of myself.
（我已經夠大了，可以照顧我自己。）

▶ The price is high enough for me to sell.
（價錢夠高了，我覺得可以賣了。）

Neither will I.
（我也不會。）

* 對方聲明不會做某事，答者說「我也不會」時，若對方用未來式的 will，答者就用 "Neither will I."。

▶ **A** If it's too hot, I will not go outside.
（要是太熱的話，我就不到外面去。）

B Neither will I.
（我也不要。）

Since nobody will participate, neither will I.
（既然沒有人要參加，我也不要。）

談天必用單字

computer	[kəm'pjutɚ]		電腦
snow	[sno]	v. 下雪；n. 雪	
ice	[aɪs]	v. 下冰；n. 冰	
unemployment	[ʌn‚ɪm'plɔɪmənt]		失業
rate	[ret]		比率
rise	[raɪz]		升高
participate	[pɚ'tɪsəpet]		參加
frozen	[frozn̩]	a. 凍結的	

談天必用片語

as long as	只要
take care of	照顧

Unit

MP3-10

The wind is really frightening.
（風勢真的很可怕。）

談論颱風

A We had to cut our vacation short because of the hurricane in Florida.
（因為佛羅里達刮颱風，我們必須縮短我們的假期。）

B That's terrible.
（真糟糕。）

Where were you?
（當時你在哪裏？）

A Right where it was coming ashore.
（就在颱風登陸的地方。）

It was getting pretty scary.
（好恐怖喲。）

B I can imagine.
（我想像得到。）

When I was in high school, a hurricane hit about five miles up the coast.

（我還在唸高中的時候，在接近我們沿海五英里的地方也刮了一次颶風。）

The wind is really frightening.
（那個風真是可怕。）

A What I don't understand is all those going out fishing in it.

（我不能了解為什麼還有人冒著颶風出去釣魚。）

B Neither do I.

（我也不了解。）

They risk their lives for a few big fish.
（他們冒著生命危險，只不過為了釣幾條大魚。）

句型靈活應用

・ **某件事很可怕，怎麼說？**

That's terrible.
（那真恐怖。）

・ **別人描述某件事，你如何表示你可以想像得到？**

I can imagine.
（我想像得到。）

・ **有人冒生命危險去做某事**

They risk their lives for a few waves.
（他們冒著生命危險，只不過為了看幾個大浪。）

Those kids risk their lives for a few dollars.
（那些小孩冒著生命危險只不過為了賺幾塊錢。）

文法句型練習

> It's getting ＋形容詞
> （漸漸地～；變得～）

* 以下例句中，形容詞之前的 pretty 是副詞，是「相當地」的意思。

▶ It's getting pretty scary.
（情況變得很嚇人。）

▶ It's getting dark.
（天漸漸暗下來了。）

▶ He is getting pretty upset.
（他已經非常憤怒。）

▶ The noise is getting louder.
（嘈雜聲越來越大。）

> 主詞＋ be 動詞＋ really ＋表示情緒的現在分詞
> （～相當地～）

* 這個句型裏，用「現在分詞」當形容詞，主詞必須是「事物」，而不是人。形容詞前面的 really 是副詞，做「相當地」的意思，用來加強形容詞。

▶ The wind is really frightening.
（風真的很嚇人。）

▶ The story is really interesting.
（這個故事真的很有趣。）

▶ The movie is really thrilling.
（這部電影真的很緊張。）

> Neither do I.
> （我也不。）

* 對方說「不」，答者也跟著說「不」時，若對方用現在簡單式，答者要用 "Neither do I."。

▶ A:I don't like him.
（我不喜歡他。）

▶ B:Neither do I.
（我也不喜歡。）

談天必用單字

vacation	[ve'keʃən]	休假；放假
hurricane	['hɝɪ,ken]	颶風；暴風
ashore	[ə'ʃor]	adv.（向）岸上
coast	[kost]	海岸
scary	['skɛrɪ]	害怕的
imagine	[ɪ'mædʒɪn]	想像
risk	[rɪsk]	v. 冒著危險
wave	[wev]	n. 海浪
thrill	[θrɪl]	v. 驚險；令人興奮

談天必用片語

cut something short	縮短
because of	因為

Unit

MP3-11

This is great kite flying weather.
（這種天放風箏最好。）

Chapter 2 美語晴雨計

看氣象，是否風大或是會下雨？

A This is great kite flying weather.
（這種天氣放風箏最好了。）

B You're right.
（你說得對。）
Check out the flags over there.
（你看那邊的旗幟。）

A Nice and steady and straight out.
（嗯，又平又穩，旗面又直。）

B Of course, but it will probably quit soon.
（當然啦，不過風也許很快就會停。）

A I don't think so.
（我想不會。）

But look at those clouds coming in.
（看看那些雲漸漸朝這邊過來了。）

B I see them.

（我看到了。）

The wind won't be dying off.
（風是不會停。）

But the rain is going to start pouring down.
（不過雨很快就會下下來。）

（句型靈活應用）

· **這是做某事最好的天氣，怎麼說？**

This is great fishing weather.

（今天真是個釣魚的好天氣。）

This is great swimming weather.

（今天真是個游泳的好天氣。）

· **對別人的意見表示不同意，怎麼說？**

A John will be our new manager.

（約翰會是我們的新經理。）

B I don't think so.

（我看不是。）

· **同意別人的看法，怎麼說？**

A Mary will be late again.

（瑪麗又要遲到了。）

B You're right.

（你說得對。）

文法句型練習

> Look at ＋受詞＋現在分詞
> （看～正在～）

＊ look at 是「感官動詞」，後面接了受詞，可再接原形動詞或現在分詞。若接現在分詞，是表示強調看著某件事正在進行。

▶ Look at those clouds coming in.

（你看那些雲朝這邊過來了。）

▶ Look at the children running to Santa Clause.

（你看那些小孩跑到聖誕老人那兒去了。）

▶ Look at the dog chasing the cat.

（你看那隻狗一直在追那隻貓。）

> start ＋動名詞
> （開始～）

＊ start 後面的動詞用動名詞 (Ving) 或不定詞 (to) 都可以，表示開始做後面這個動作。

▶ The rain is going to start pouring down.

（雨很快就會下下來了。）

▶ When are you going to start doing your homework?

（你什麼時候才會開始做你的功課呀？）

▶You'd better start working out.
（你最好開始做健身運動。）

談天必用單字

weather	[ˈwɛðɚ]	天氣
steady	[ˈstɛdɪ]	很穩定的
straight	[stret]	很直的
pour	[por]	傾盆而降
manager	[ˈmænɪdʒɚ]	經理
chase	[tʃes]	追趕

談天必用片語

die off		漸漸消失
pour down		傾盆而降
check out		查看

Chapter 3

健身美語

Unit

MP3-12

I've got to start working out.
（我必須開始做健身運動。）

談論如何健身

A I've got to start working out.

（我必須開始做健身運動了。）

B Me too.

（我也是。）

I've gained ten pounds this year.
（今年我重了十磅。）

A It's not the weight that bothers me.

（我煩惱的不是體重。）

It's the flab.
（而是肌肉鬆弛。）

B Really? What are you going to do?

（真的嗎？那你要怎麼辦？）

A Probably go to the gym and use the weight

machines.

（我只能回到健身房去做做舉重。）

B Yuck. I think I will try swimming.

（舉重，我才不要，我想我要游泳。）

句型靈活應用

- **我真的必須做某事，怎麼說？**

I've got to start working out.

（我必須開始做做運動了。）

I've got to get some more chemicals.

（我必須多吃一點維他命之類的東西。）

I've got to find another way home.

（我必須想個別的辦法回家。）

- **表示我也是，怎麼說？**

A I've got to go now.

（我現在必須離開了。）

B Me too.

（我也是。）

- **長胖了怎麼說？**

I've gained ten pounds this year.

（我今年重了十磅。）

I've gained weight lately.

（我最近胖了。）

> try ＋動名詞
> （嘗試～）

＊ try 後面接動名詞(Ving)或不定詞(to)意思不同：若是接動名詞，表示把後面這個動作當實驗，嘗試做看看；若加不定詞，表示「盡力去做」這件事，但做得成不成功就不一定了。

▶ I will try swimming.
（我要試試游泳。）

▶ I will try biking.
（我要試試騎自行車。）

▶ I will try talking to him.
（我要試著跟他講話。）

談天必用單字

bother	[ˈbɑðɚ]	煩惱
weight	[wet]	重量
machine	[məˈʃin]	機器
probably	[ˈprɑbəblɪ]	也許
flab	[flæb]	肌肉鬆弛
chemicals	[ˈkɛmɪklz]	化學合成品

談天必用片語

work out		健身

Unit

12

MP3-13

Biking is a good way to get some exercises.
（騎腳踏車是運動的好方法。）

騎腳踏車做運動

Ⓐ Is that a new bike you have?
（那是你新買的腳踏車嗎？）

Ⓑ Yes, biking is a good way to get some exercises.
（是的，騎腳踏車是運動的好方法。）

Ⓐ Do you ride with your children?
（你跟你的小孩一道騎嗎？）

Ⓑ Yes. We go all over the bike trails down by the lake.
（是的，我們到湖邊的自行車道四處去騎。）

Ⓐ That sounds like fun.
（聽起來好像很有趣。）
Maybe I'll try it one day.
（也許有一天我會試一下。）

句型靈活應用

· 有人給你建議，你有意一試，怎麼說？

Maybe I'll try it one day. （也許有一天我會試一下。）

Maybe I'll give it a try. （也許有一天我會試試看。）

- 看到別人的新東西時，你該如何打開話題？

Is that a new bike you have?
（那是你的新車嗎？）

Is that a new car you have?
（那是你新買的車嗎？）

文法句型練習

動名詞＋動詞

* 「動名詞」就是 "動詞(V)+ing"，它的用法跟名詞一樣，可以當主詞或受詞用。

▶ Biking is a good way to get some exercises.
（騎自行車是運動的好方法。）

▶ Working on computers is his hobby.
（玩電腦是他的嗜好。）

談天必用單字

exercise	[ˈɛksɚˌsaɪz]	運動
computer	[kəmˈpjutɚ]	電腦
hobby	[ˈhɑbɪ]	嗜好
bike	[baɪk]	自行車
trail	[trel]	小路

談天必用片語

work on		工作

Unit

13

MP3-14

I don't like sit-ups.

（我不喜歡做仰臥起坐。）

談健身錄影帶

A Have you seen that new exercise video?

（你有沒有看到那卷新的健身錄影帶？）

B Yes. It's a lot more advanced than anything I can do right now.

（有呀。那裏面的動作比我現在做的更高級。）

A It's more advanced than anything I'd want to do.

（那裏面的動作比我「願意」做的更高級。）

B This is true.

（那是實在話。）

They have you do different kinds of leg lifts.
（他們叫你做不同的舉腳運動。）

A And different types of sit-ups.

（還有不同的仰臥起坐。）

B And if there is anything worse than leg lifts, it's sit-ups!

（是呀，如果還有什麼比舉腳運動還難的，那就是仰臥起坐了。）

句型靈活應用

・ **問對方有沒有看過某件新東西，來打開話題**

Have you seen that new exercise video?
（你有沒有看過那卷新的健身錄影帶？）

Have you seen that new movie?
（你有沒有看過那部新電影？）

Have you seen Mary's new dress?
（你有沒有看過瑪麗的新衣服？）

・ **某件事比另一件事更糟，怎麼說？**

If there is anything worse than leg lifts, it's sit-ups!
（如果還有什麼比舉腳還難的，就是仰臥起坐了。）

If there is anything worse than English class, it's Math class.
（如果還有什麼比英語課還難，那就是數學了。）

句型練習

A is more ＋形容詞 than B
（A 比 B 更～）

＊ 形容詞的比較級有兩種方式，其一是在形容詞前面加 more，這種用法大半是形容詞本身為多音節，例如 expensive「昂貴」和 advanced「先進」。

▶ A pen is more expensive than a pencil.
（鋼筆比鉛筆貴。）

▶ My English class is more advanced than his.
（我的英語課比他的高級。）

> A is more ＋形容詞 than anything 某人 can ～.
> （A 比某人現在能做的更～）

＊ 比較級不一定比較 A 和 B 兩件東西。本句型是以一件事去比較某人現在所能做的任何事。

▶ It's a lot more advanced than anything I can do right now.
（那裏面的東西比我現在能做的還要高級許多。）

▶ The piano music is more difficult than anything I can play right now.
（這首鋼琴曲比我現在能彈奏的更困難。）

> A is more ＋形容詞 than anything
> 某人 would like to ～.
> （A 比某人願意做的更～）

＊ 本句型是以一件事去比較某人願意做的任何事。

▶ It's more advanced than anything I'd want to do.
（那裏面的東西比我願意做的還高級。）

▶ The price is higher than what I'd like to pay.
（那個價錢比我願意付的還要高。）

Chapter 3 健身美語

51

> have ＋受詞＋原形動詞
> （要某人做～）

＊ have 是「使役動詞」，加受詞之後要再加原形動詞。

▶ **They have you do different kinds of leg lifts.**
（他們讓你做各種不同的舉腳運動。）

▶ **They have me do all the typing work.**
（他們叫我做所有的打字工作。）

談天必用單字

video	[ˈvɪdio]	錄影帶
lift	[lɪft]	抬起來
sit-up	[ˈsɪtˌʌp]	仰臥起坐
advanced	[ədˈvænst]	高級的
different	[ˈdɪfərənt]	不同的
kind	[kaɪnd]	n. 種類；adj. 仁慈的
difficult	[ˈdɪfəkʌlt]	困難
expensive	[ɪksˈpɛnsɪv]	昂貴的

談天必用片語

right now	現在
different kinds of	不同種類的
different types of	不同樣式的

Unit

I got an exercise machine.
（我買了一個運動器材。）

談購買運動器材

A I see you got an exercise machine.
（我看見你新買了一個運動器材。）
How do you like it?
（你覺得怎麼樣？）

B Well, I really needed to start exercising.
（我實在真的需要做做運動了。）
It's O.K.
（這個器材還不錯。）
I use it while I watch the news.
（我一邊看電視新聞一邊使用。）

A I was wondering when you would find the time.
（我還在想你怎麼會有時間呢。）

B It sure beats going to the gym.
（總是比到健身房去要好。）
You don't waste time going to and from.
（你不需要浪費時間來回。）

A Yes, but I think I'll stick with the gym.
（那是真的，不過我想我還是會到健身房去。）

句型靈活應用

· **對某事感到很不了解，怎麼說？**

I was wondering when you would find the time.
（我還在想你怎麼會有時間呢。）

I was wondering why he would marry her.
（我還在想他為什麼會跟她結婚。）

· **說某事肯定比另一件事還好，怎麼說？**

Swimming in the swimming pool sure beats going to the beach.
（在游泳池裏面游泳肯定比到海邊去要好。）

Going to a movie sure beats watching TV.
（看電影肯定比看電視要好。）

文法句型練習

> Waste time (by) ＋動名詞
> （因～浪費時間）

* 以下句型中，waste time 後面省略掉一個介系詞 "by"，所以後面
接的是「動名詞」。例如:going 和 talking。

▶You don't waste time going to and from.
（你不用費時往返。）

▶ Don't waste time talking on the phone all the time.
（不要一直浪費時間講電話。）

┌─────────────────────┐
│ I see that ＋子句   │
│ （我看到～）   │
└─────────────────────┘

＊ I see 後面帶出一個子句，表示你所看到的事情。that 可以省略
掉。

▶ I see you got an exercise machine.
（我看見你買了一個運動器材。）

▶ I see that you got a new computer.
（我看見你買了一台新電腦。）

▶ I see that you worked very hard.
（我看見你工作很認真。）

談天必用單字

wonder	[ˈwʌndɚ]	懷疑
beat	[bit]	勝過
waste	[west]	浪費

談天必用片語

to and from	往返
find the time	找時間
wait in line	排隊等候
stick with	堅持
go to a movie	看電影
all the time	一直

Unit

15

MP3-16

A little exercise would do you good.
（做點運動對你有好處。）

談論做運動的時機

A I really think a little exercise would do you good.
（我真的覺得做點運動對你有好處。）

B Well, maybe.
（是嗎，也許吧。）
But I don't have the time to go to a gym.
（但是我沒有時間到健身房去。）

A You don't have to.
（你不用去的。）
You can walk or ride a bike.
（你可以散步或騎自行車。）

B I don't have a bike.
（可是我沒有自行車，）
And it's too hot to walk.
（而且散步的話太熱了。）

A Look, you work on the 8th floor.
（這樣吧，你在八樓上班，）
You can just walk up and down the stairs.
（你可以走路上下樓。）

That would beat any exercise machine.
（那可比什麼運動器材都要好。）
The stairs is inside and air-conditioned.
（而且樓梯在房間裏面，又有冷氣。）
And you'll save time not waiting for the elevator.
（你又可以節省等電梯的時間。）

B Well, you've got a point there.
（噢，你説得蠻有道理的。）

句型靈活應用

· 說某事對你有好處，怎麼說？

A little exercise would do you good.
（做些運動對你有好處。）

Eight glasses of water a day would do you good.
（一天八杯水對你有好處。）

Taking a walk every day would do you good.
（每天散步對你有好處。）

· 說某人說的話有道理

You've got a point there.
（你説得有道理。）

文法句型練習

Save time（by）not ＋動名詞
（因不做～而節省時間）

* Save time 後面也有個介系詞 "by" 省略掉，所以後面的動詞要改為「動名詞」，例如以下例句中的 waiting 和 wasting。

▶ You'll save time not waiting for the elevator.
（你可以節省等電梯的時間。）

▶ You'll be better off not wasting your money on smoking.
（你如果不浪費錢在抽煙上，你會更有錢。）

> too ＋形容詞＋ to ＋原形動詞
> （太～而不能～）

▶ It's too hot to walk.
（散步的話太熱了。）

▶ It's too hard to explain.
（這很難去解釋。）

談天必用單字

stairs	[stɛrz]	樓梯
elevator	[ˈɛləˌvetɚ]	電梯
explain	[ɪksˈplen]	解釋
air-conditioned	[ˌɛrkənˈdɪʃənd]	冷氣
point	[pɔɪnt]	重點

談天必用片語

save time	節省時間
wait for	等待
up and down	上下

Chapter 4

運動美語

Unit

16

MP3-17

We're going to the baseball game.
（我們要去看棒球賽。）

談看球賽

A John is going to take the kids to the baseball game on Friday.
（約翰這個禮拜五要帶小孩去看棒球賽。）

B That game has been sold out for weeks.
（那場球賽的門票幾個禮拜之前就賣光了。）
How did he get tickets?
（那他是怎麼拿到票的？）

A His brother's company has a box at the stadium.
（他哥哥的公司在球場有一個包廂。）
And it happens to be his weekend to use it.
（這個周末剛好輪到他哥哥使用。）

B That's great.
（那太好了。）
What is the box like?
（球場的包廂怎樣？）

A To start with, it is air-conditioned.
（首先，那兒有冷氣。）

They also have all sorts of food and drinks available.
（裏面又有各種吃的喝的。）

B That sounds great.
（那太好了。）

句型靈活應用

- **說某件事真好，怎麼說？**

  That's great.
  （那太好了。）

  That sounds great.
  （聽起來很好。）

- **票已經賣光了，怎麼說？**

  That game has been sold out for weeks.
  （那場球賽的門票好幾個禮拜前就賣光了。）

  Is the concert sold out?
  （音樂會的票賣光了嗎？）

- **碰巧輪到誰，怎麼說？**

  It happens to be his weekend to use it.
  （這個周末剛好輪到他使用。）

  It happens to be your turn to do the dishes.
  （這回剛好輪到你洗碗。）

文法句型練習

> How did ＋主詞＋原形動詞？
> （某人如何～？）

＊ 詢問做成一件事的方法，疑問詞用 How。

▶ **How did he get tickets?**
（他是怎麼拿到票的？）

▶ **How did you get here?**
（你是怎麼到那裏的？）

▶ **How did she know my address?**
（她怎麼會知道我的住址呢？）

> That sounds ＋形容詞
> That sounds like ＋名詞
> （聽起來好像～）

＊ sound 後面要接形容詞；若是用 sound like，後面要接名詞。

▶ **That sounds great.**
（那聽起來很好。）

▶ **That sounds interesting.**
（那聽起來很有意思。）

▶ **That sounds like fun.**
（那聽起來好像很有趣。）

談天必用單字

ticket	[ˈtɪkɪt]	票
company	[ˈkʌmpənɪ]	公司
stadium	[ˈstedɪəm]	球場
air-conditioned	[ˌɛrkənˈdɪʃənd]	有冷氣的
sort	[sɔrt]	種類

談天必用片語

to start with	首先

Unit

17

MP3-18

Mary joined the swim team.
（瑪麗參加游泳隊。）

談參加游泳隊以及練習時間

Ⓐ Mary joined the swim team this summer.
（瑪麗今年夏天參加游泳隊。）

Ⓑ Really? How does she like it?
（真的嗎？她喜歡嗎？）

Ⓐ I think she is enjoying it.
（我想她還喜歡。）

But she isn't too wild about the seven a.m. practices.
（不過，她對早上 7 點就要練習不太高興。）

Ⓑ I wouldn't be wild about them, either.
（早上 7 點就要練習我也不會太高興。）

How does she get there?
（她怎麼去？）

A She takes the bus.
（她搭巴士。）

- **問對某件事情的看法**

How does she like it?
（她還喜歡嗎？）

How do you like the show?
（你喜不喜歡這個表演？）

- **表示對某事不是那麼狂熱**

She isn't too wild about the seven a.m.
practices.
（她對早上 7 點就要練習不太高興。）

She's not too wild about the movie.
（她對那部電影不是很熱衷。）

I'm not too wild about playing Mahjong all
night.
（我對整個晚上打麻將不太熱衷。）

文法句型練習

I think ＋子句
　（我認為～。）

＊ I think 後面帶出一個子句，表示「我所認為」的事情。

▶ I think she is enjoying it.
（我想她還蠻喜歡的。）

▶ I think she is enjoying your company.
（我想她對跟你一道去還蠻喜歡的。）

▶ I think he would be all right.
（我想他應該沒有問題。）

> I wouldn't be ＋形容詞＋, ＋ either.
> （我也不會～）

＊ 對方說「我不會」，答者說「我也不會」時，可用 "I wouldn't be ～ , either."

▶ There is another typhoon coming.
（又有一個颱風要來了。）

▶ But, I'm not too worried about it.
（不過，我不太擔心。）

▶ I wouldn't be too worried about it, either.
（我也不太擔心。）

談天必用單字

wild	[waɪld]	狂熱
practice	[ˈpræktɪs]	練習
company	[ˈkʌmpənɪ]	陪伴

談天必用片語

| take the bus | | 搭巴士 |

Unit

18

MP3-19

He is in the football team.
（他在足球隊。）

與朋友談兒子

A Is John going for football this year?
（約翰今年要打美式足球嗎？）

B Yes, he's hoping to make the team.
（是的，他希望能夠被選入校隊。）

A Is this the first year he'd play?
（這是他第一年打嗎？）

B No, he played last year a little.
（不，他去年打了一點。）
He has really grown recently.
（他最近長得好高了。）

A That's true.
（那是真的。）
I almost didn't recognize him last week at the

grocery.

（我上個禮拜在雜貨店看到他都快要認不得了。）

B He's easy to recognize at the grocery.

（在雜貨店裏他最好認了。）

He's the one eating his way through the store!
（那個在店裏一路吃東西的就是他。）

句型靈活應用

- **表示差一點怎麼樣，怎麼說？**

I almost didn't recognize him.
（我幾乎認不出他了。）

I almost missed the bus.
（我差一點就趕不上這班巴士。）

- **說某人在某段時間一直做某件事，怎麼說？**

He always eats his way through the store.
（他在店裏總是一路吃個不停。）

The girl next to me talked through the whole movie.
（坐我旁邊的女孩整場電影一直都在講話。）

- **說某人就是那個做某件事的人，怎麼說？**

He's the one eating his way through the store.
（他就是那個在店裏一路吃東西的人。）

She's the one falling asleep during the

meeting.

（她就是那位在開會時睡著的小姐。）

> He's hoping to ＋原形動詞
> （他正期待著～）

* 他「正」期待著，用現在進行式的語法 "be+Ving"，表示持續的、一直的期待。

▶ **He's hoping to make the team.**
（他一直希望能入選校隊。）

▶ **He's hoping to ace the English exam.**
（他一直希望英語測驗能考個「A」。）

recognize	[ˈrɛkəgnaɪz]	最近的
recently	[ˈrisəntlɪ]	認識
grocery	[ˈɡrosərɪ]	雜貨店
ace	[es]	拿「A」

make the team	入選代表隊
last year	去年
a little	一些

Unit

19

MP3-20

Congratulations on making the tennis team.

（恭喜你被選入網球隊。）

談被選為網球選手

A Hey, congratulations on making the tennis team.

（嗨，恭喜你入選網球代表隊。）

B Thanks. I've been practicing all year.

（謝謝了，我一整年都在練習。）

A Well, I'm sure you'll do great.

（是嗎，我確定你的表現一定很好。）

B I just hope I win at least one match.

（我只希望我最少贏一場球。）

A Look, if the coaches didn't think you could win, you wouldn't have made the team.

（看吧，如果教練認為你不能贏球，你就不可能被選入代表隊。）

B I'm just really nervous about the match tomorrow.

（我只是很緊張明天的比賽。）

· 恭喜對方的成就，怎麼說？

Congratulations on making the tennis team.
（恭喜你入選網球代表隊。）

Congratulations on winning the first place.
（恭喜你贏得第一名。）

· 以不很確定的說法，說一件事

I guess you're right.
（我想你是對的。）

I guess his company is going out of business.
（我猜他的公司就要關門了。）

· 以很肯定的語氣，說一件事

I'm sure you'll do great.
（我確定你會表現得很好。）

I'm sure he'll become famous.
（我確定他一定會出名。）

> If ＋主詞＋動詞過去式，＋主詞＋ would ＋ have ＋過去分詞
> （如果～，就～）

＊ 本句型是與「過去事實相反」的假設法語氣。

▶ If the coaches didn't think you could win, you wouldn't have made the team.
（如果教練不認為你會贏，你就不會入選代表隊。）

▶ If you didn't practice so hard, you wouldn't have won the first place.
（如果你不那麼認真練習的話，你就不可能贏得第一名。）

> 主詞＋ have ＋ been ＋現在分詞
> （一直都～）

＊ 本句型是現在完成進行式的用法，表示從過去到現在一直都在做。

▶ I've been practicing all year.
（我一整年都在練習。）

▶ I've been working on the project for three years.
（這個專案我已經做了三年了。）

談天必用單字

practice	[ˈpræktɪs]	練習
match	[mætʃ]	比賽

coach	[kotʃ]	教練
nervous	[ˈnɝvəs]	緊張
project	[ˈprɑdʒɛkt]	專案
famous	[ˈfeməs]	出名

談天必用片語

at least		至少
work on		工作
out of business		倒閉
the first place		第一名
congratulations	[kəngrætʃəˈleʃənz]	恭喜

Chapter 5

個人嗜好

Unit

20

MP3-21

I'm doing some needlework.
（我在做針線。）

談做針線

A **What are you working on?**
（你在做什麼？）

B **I'm doing some embroidery.**
（我在做一點刺繡。）

A **I didn't know you did needlework.**
（我不知道你也會做針線。）

B **I don't very much, just for very special occasions.**
（我不常做，只在特殊場合才做。）

I don't have the time to do it all the time, you know.
（你知道我是沒有時間常做針線的。）

- **詢問別人在做什麼？**

  What are you working on?

  （你正在做什麼？）

  What are you doing?

  （你正在做什麼？）

* 問對方正在做哪一件工作，用 work on；若只是隨意問對方在
做什麼事，就用 do。

- **沒有時間做某事，怎麼說？**

  I don't have the time to do it all the time.

  （我沒有時間可以一直這樣做。）

  I don't have the time to watch TV.

  （我沒有時間看電視。）

  I don't have the time to go to the gym.

  （我沒時間上健身房。）

文法句型練習

> I didn't know ＋子句
> （我不知道～）

* I didn't know 後面帶出一個子句，表示「我所不知道的事」。

▶ **I didn't know you did needlework.**

（我不知道你會做針線。）

▶ I didn't know she played the piano.
（我不知道她會彈鋼琴。）

談天必用單字

embroidery	[ɪmˈbrɔɪdərɪ]	刺繡
needlework	[ˈnidl̩ˌwɝk]	針線
special	[ˈspɛʃəl]	特殊
occasion	[əˈkeʒən]	場合

談天必用片語

all the time	一直

76

Unit

MP3-22

She plays the piano very well.
（她鋼琴彈得很好。）

談論朋友的音樂天分

A John is getting Mary a grand piano for their anniversary.

（約翰送瑪麗一台演奏型鋼琴作為他們的結婚紀念。）

B Really?

（真的？）

I didn't know she played.
（我不知道她會彈琴。）

A She is really quite talented.

（她很有天分。）

But she just plays to relax.
（不過，她彈琴只是為了舒展身心。）

B I know she sings well.

（我知道她很會唱歌。）

Does she play well also?

（她也很會彈琴嗎？）

A Very well!

（彈得很好喲！）

B Wow! Maybe we can talk her into doing a concert for us.

（哇，也許我們可以說服她為我們開個音樂會。）

句型靈活應用

・ 說某人要買一件東西送給某人，怎麼說？

John is getting Mary a grand piano for their anniversary.

（約翰送瑪麗一台演奏型鋼琴作為結婚紀念。）

My dad is getting me a stereo for my birthday.

（我爸爸送我一套音響作為我的生日禮物。）

Are you getting me a new car for my birthday?

（我過生日的時候你要送我一部新車嗎？）

・ 說服某人去做某事，怎麼說？

Maybe we can talk her into doing a concert for us.

（也許我們可以說服她為我們開個音樂會。）

Maybe I can talk her into joining our team.

（也許我可以說服她加入我們的隊伍。）

You can't talk me into playing tennis with you.
（你不能説服我跟你一起打網球。）

＊ 注意 "talk 某人 into" 的後面要接動名詞。

> 動詞＋副詞
> （做得很～）

＊ 要說明一個動作的狀態或程度，要用副詞去修飾動詞。例如下面句中的 well 就是修飾 sing 和 play 的副詞，表示「唱得很好」和「彈得很好」。

▶ I know she sings well.
（我知道她唱得很好。）

▶ Does she play well also?
（她也彈得很好嗎？）

談天必用單字

grand	[grænd]	大的
anniversary	[͵ænɪ'vɝsərɪ]	結婚紀念日
talented	['tæləntɪd]	有天分的
relax	[rɪ'læks]	舒展身心
concert	['kɑnsɚt]	音樂會

談天必用片語

talk into~		說服

Chapter 5
個人嗜好

Unit

22

MP3-23

I like to play the guitar.

（我喜歡彈吉他。）

談如何學會彈吉他

A Where did you learn to play the guitar?
（你在什麼地方學會彈吉它的？）

B I just taught myself.
（我是自己教自己，無師自通。）

A Really?
（真的嗎？）
You read the music and figured out what the cords are?
（你可以讀樂譜，然後判斷彈什麼和弦嗎？）

B No, I don't know how to read music.
（不，我不會讀樂譜。）
I just listen to songs on the radio.
（我是從收音機聽歌曲。）
And then play them until they sound right.
（然後一直彈，彈到聽起來無誤為止。）

A You're kidding?
（你在開玩笑吧？）

B No, really.
（不，真的。）

I'll buy a tape and listen to it over and over.
（我通常買一卷錄音帶，反覆一遍又一遍的聽。）

And then, I can play.
（然後我就會彈了。）

Just like that.
（就是這樣而已。）

句型靈活應用

· **在肯定句句尾加問號，表示因「不能確定」而追問**

You read the music and figured out what the cords are?
（你可以看樂譜，然後判斷彈什麼和弦嗎？）

You're kidding?
（你在開玩笑吧？）

You didn't go to work today?
（你今天沒有上班嗎？）

· **談看樂譜**

A You have to read the music before you'd play the guitar.
（在你彈吉他之前一定要看樂譜。）

B But I don't know how to read music.
（可是我不會看樂譜。）

＊ 「看樂譜」的英文說法是 "read music"，但特指某一首曲子的樂

譜時，用 "read the music"。

・說某件事就是那樣子，沒什麼

Just like that.

（就是那樣而已。）

Where did you ＋主詞＋原形動詞？
（你從哪裏～？）

＊ 問「哪裏」的疑問句要用 where。

► Where did you learn to play the guitar?
（你在哪裏學會彈吉他的？）

► Where did you learn to swim?
（你在哪裏學會游泳的？）

► Where did you get the news?
（你在哪裏得到的消息？）

I don't know how to ＋原形動詞
（我不知道如何～？）

＊ how to 加上動詞，做 "I don't know" 的受詞，表示「我不知道該如何做」。

► I don't know how to read music.
（我不知道如何看樂譜。）

► I don't know how to play the guitar.
（我不知道如何彈吉他。）

► I don't know how to swim.
（我不知道如何游泳。）

主詞＋ figure out ＋疑問子句
　　（某人能理解或想出來～）

＊ 「疑問子句」做 figure out 的受詞時，要用肯定句型，不是疑問
　　句型。例如下句用 "what the cords are"，而不是 "what are the
　　cords"。

► I figured out what the cords are.
（我可以想出來用什麼和弦。）

► He figured out what the password is.
（他終於猜到通行口令。）

► I figured out why they would say that.
（我想到他們為什麼會這樣說。）

談天必用單字

figure	[ˈfɪgjɚ]	想出來
cord	[kɔrd]	和弦
password	[ˈpæswɚd]	通行口令

談天必用片語

figure out		想出來
listen to		聆聽
over and over		一遍又一遍
read music		看樂譜

Unit

23

MP3-24

Do you do pottery?
（你平時做陶器嗎？）

談論做陶瓷

A Do you do pottery?
（你做陶器嗎？）

B Yes, both pottery and ceramics.
（是的，我做陶器和瓷器。）

A What is the difference between the two?
（它們兩種有什麼不同嗎？）

B Just the type of clay that's used.
（它們的不同在於使用的土種類不同。）

A Doing pottery looked like fun.
（做陶器好像很有趣的樣子。）

B Would you like to try it?
（你要不要試一下？）

A Boy, would I? Thanks.
（哇，讓我試呀？謝謝。）

- **表示不敢相信，怎麼說？**

  A Would you like to try it?
  （你要不要試一下？）

  B Boy, would I?
  （哇，讓我來試呀？）

> 動名詞當主詞
> （做～）

* 「動名詞」的用法與「名詞」相同，所以可以做主詞。

▶ Doing pottery looked like fun.
（做陶器好像很有趣。）

▶ Playing the guitar looked like fun.
（彈吉他好像很有趣。）

pottery	[ˈpɑtɚɪ]	陶瓷
ceramics	[səˈræmɪks]	陶器
difference	[ˈdɪfərəns]	不同
clay	[kle]	黏土

| would like | | 想要 |

Chapter 5 個人嗜好

Unit

24

MP3-25

I've taken up photography.
（我在學攝影。）

談論攝影和沖洗照片

A I've got to get some more chemicals.
（我必須添購一些化學藥品。）

B What do you need chemicals for?
（你要化學藥品做什麼？）

A I've taken up photography and have set up a darkroom.
（我現在在學攝影，而且設了一間暗房。）

B I tried photography for a while.
（我曾經試過攝影一陣子。）

But it was too expensive to have them developed.
（但是沖洗照片太貴了。）

A If you are interested, I would be willing to develop the film for you.
（如果你有興趣的話，我很樂意幫你沖照片。）

B I might do that. Thanks.
（我可能會這樣做，謝謝你。）

句型靈活應用

- **問對方為何需要那件東西，怎麼說？**

    A May I borrow your typewriter?
    （我可以借用你的打字機嗎？）

    B What do you need it for?
    （你要打字機做什麼？）

- **表示可能做某事，怎麼說？**

    I might do that.
    （我可能這樣做。）

    I might try it.
    （我可能會試一下。）

    I might enter the beauty pageant.
    （我可能會參加選美比賽。）

文法句型練習

> If ＋主詞＋現在式動詞，＋主詞＋ will（would）＋原形動詞
> （如果～，我願意～）

＊ 本句型不是「假設法語氣」，只是單純地說明一件可能發生的事。

▶ If you are interested, I would be willing to develop the film for you.
（如果你有興趣的話，我很樂意為你沖洗照片。）

▶ If I find your purse, I'll give it to you.
（如果我找到你的錢包，我會把它還給你。）

> have ＋受詞＋過去分詞
> （使～被～）

＊ 使役動詞 have 的受詞之後加過去分詞表示「被動」。

▶ It was too expensive to have them developed.
（沖洗照片太貴了。）

▶ I'll have my car washed.
（我要把車洗一下。）

▶ Something is wrong with my car. I'll have it fixed by a mechanic.
（我的車子有毛病，我要找個修車工修理一下。）

談天必用單字

photography	[fə'tɑgrəfɪ]	攝影
darkroom	['dɑrkrum]	暗房
develop	[dɪ'vɛləp]	沖洗
film	[fɪlm]	底片
mechanic	[mə'kænɪk]	修車工 學習
chemical	['kɛmɪkl̩]	化學藥品

談天必用片語

take up	學習
set up	設立
be willing to	很樂意

Chapter 6

喜慶社交

Unit

25

MP3-26

Mary's baby shower is this week.
（這個星期瑪麗要做嬰兒祝福禮。）

談論要送什麼嬰兒禮物

A Mary's baby shower is this week.
（這個星期瑪麗要做嬰兒祝福禮。）
What are you getting her?
（你要送她什麼？）

B I don't know.
（我還不知道。）
Do they know whether it is a boy or girl?
（他們知道嬰兒是男的還是女的？）

A No, they don't.
（不，他們還不知道。）

B Oh well, it's easier to pick out something when you know the sex.
（噢，要是知道性別的話就比較好選東西。）
What are you getting her?
（你要送她什麼？）

A I am knitting a green and yellow blanket for the baby.

（我正在幫嬰兒織一條綠色配黃色的毯子。）

It's almost finished.

（快要織完了。）

B How nice!

（這樣太好了。）

I guess I'd better head to the store.

（我想我最好趕快去店裏買了。）

* "baby shower" 是在嬰兒出生之前，朋友們送給準媽媽的祝福禮。

句型靈活應用

・ **某個聚會在何時舉行，怎麼說？**

Mary's baby shower is this week.

（這個禮拜瑪麗要做嬰兒祝福禮。）

John's wedding is next week.

（約翰的婚禮在下個禮拜。）

・ **送某人何種禮物，怎麼說？**

What are you getting her?

（你要送她什麼東西？）

I'm getting him a computer.

（我要送他一部電腦。）

My dad is getting me a car.

（我爸爸送我一輛車。）

- **某件事快做完了，怎麼說？**

It's almost finished.
（事情快要做完了。）

The project is almost finished.
（整個專案快要做完了。）

My homework is almost finished.
（我的功課快要做完了。）

> Do you know whether ～ ?
> 　（你知道是～嗎？）

* whether 所帶出的子句正是 "Do you know" 所問的事情。

▶ Do they know whether it is a boy or girl?
（他們已經曉得是男孩還是女孩了嗎？）

▶ Do you know whether he is coming or not?
（你曉得他會不會來嗎？）

> had better ＋原形動詞
> 　（最好～）

* had better 後面要加「原形動詞」；had 通常和主詞連結縮寫。

▶ I'd better head to the store.
（我最好趕快去店裏一趟。）

▶ You'd better listen to her.

（你最好聽她的話。）

談天必用單字

shower	[ʃaʊr]	祝福禮
whether	[ˈhwɛðɚ]	是否
sex	[sɛks]	性別
knit	[nɪt]	織
blanket	[ˈblænkɪt]	毯子
wedding	[ˈwɛdɪŋ]	婚禮
project	[ˈprɑdʒɛkt]	專案

談天必用片語

pick out	選擇
had better	最好
head to	去一趟

Unit

26

MP3-27

They are having a band at their wedding reception.

（他們的婚宴上將請一個樂隊。）

談論婚宴和跳舞

A Did you know John and Mary are having a band at their wedding reception?

（你知道約翰和瑪麗的婚宴上要請一個樂團演奏嗎？）

B No, I didn't.

（不，我不知道。）

I guess I'd better get out my dancing shoes.
（我想我最好把我的舞鞋找出來。）

A It should be a lot of fun.

（這個婚宴一定很好玩。）

The band is supposed to be really good.
（他們請的樂團應該是很好的。）

B Yes!

（是呀。）

Maybe I can convince my husband to find his dancing shoes.

（也許我可以説服我先生把他的舞鞋找出來。）

I don't think we've danced since our wedding.

（自從我們結婚後，我想我們就沒有跳過舞。）

A What is the deal?

（怎麼搞的？）

Guys get married and forget how to dance?

（男人一結婚就忘記怎麼跳舞了嗎？）

B It sure seems that way.

（似乎就是這樣。）

句型靈活應用

· **問對方知不知道某件事，怎麼說？**

Did you know we are going to have a new manager?

（你曉不曉得我們會請一個新的經理？）

Did you know John failed in the entrance examination?

（你知不知道約翰入學考試沒有考上？）

· **說某件事為何會這樣，怎麼說？**

What is the deal?

（怎麼搞的？）

- 表示某事似乎就是這個樣子，怎麼說？

It sure seems that way.
（事情似乎就是這樣。）

文法句型練習

主詞＋ be 動詞＋現在分詞
（將要～）

＊ 本句型是用「現在進行式」，表示即將發生或已計劃好的事。

▶ They are having a band at their wedding reception.
（他們的婚宴上會請一個樂隊來演奏。）

▶ They are having a sale at Sogo.
（崇光百貨將舉行一個大拍賣。）

▶ We are having a piano contest next Saturday.
（我們下個禮拜六有一場鋼琴比賽。）

談天必用單字

band	[bænd]	樂團
reception	[rɪˈsɛpʃən]	接待
convince	[kənˈvɪns]	說服
forget	[fɚˈgɛt]	忘記

談天必用片語

be supposed to	應該是
a lot of	許多
get out something	找出某樣東西

Unit

We're planning a birthday party for John.
（我們正為約翰計劃生日派對。）

談生日派對

A We're planning a surprise birthday party for John.

（我們正在為約翰計劃一個秘密生日派對。）

B Really?

（真的嗎？）

How old will he be?

（過了生日他是幾歲？）

A This is the big four-oh.

（就是大大的 40 歲。）

B How is he taking it?

（他自己覺得如何？）

A I don't know.

（我不知道。）

I guess we'll find out at the party.

（我想我們在派對裏就會知道。）

B Well, I'll certainly be there to see his reaction.

（是嗎，那我一定要在那個地方看他的反應喲。）

・ 說 20, 30, 40 ～等等的數字，有時會說成 2 和英文字　母 "O"，以此類推。

How old will John be?

（約翰將滿幾歲？）

This is the big four-oh.

（就是大大的 40 歲。）

・ 某人發生事情時，問「他的反應如何？」

A John lost a lot of money in the stock market.

（約翰在股票市場損失很多錢。）

B How is he taking it?

（他自己覺得怎麼樣？）

文法句型練習

主詞＋ be 動詞＋現在分詞
　　（正在～）

＊ 本句型是現在進行式，表示正在做的事。

▶ We're planning a surprise birthday party for John.

（我們正在為約翰計劃一個秘密生日派對。）

▶ We're working on the terms with ABC company.

（我們正與 ABC 公司協調交易條件。）

> How old 〜 ?
>
> （幾歲？）

* 問幾歲，是問現在幾歲，明年幾歲，還是去年幾歲？要注意時式的不同用法。

▶ How old will he be?

（他將滿幾歲？）

▶ How old is he?

（他幾歲了？）

▶ How old are you?

（請問你今年貴庚？）

▶ How old was he when he got the doctorate degree?

（他拿到博士學位的時候是幾歲？）

談天必用單字

surprise	[sɚˈpraɪz]	驚訝
reaction	[rɪˈækʃən]	反應
certainly	[ˈsɝtənlɪ]	肯定

談天必用片語

find out		找出來、發現

Unit

28

MP3-29

They are moving next week.
（他們下星期要搬家。）

談論朋友要搬家以及送別

A The Smiths are moving next week.
（史密司一家下禮拜要搬家了。）

We are going to have a going-away party for them Saturday.
（我們打算這個禮拜六幫他們做一個餞別宴。）

B I didn't realize they were moving so soon.
（我不曉得他們這麼快就要搬家。）

They are really going to be missed.
（我們一定會記得他們的。）

A Yes, but we'll have one last chance to get together.
（是的，不過我們還有最後一次和他們相聚的機會。）

We're planning a barbecue.
（我們打算來一次烤肉。）

B That's perfect.

（那太好了。）

We've had so many impromptu barbecues with them over the years.

（這麼多年來我們都是臨時決定烤肉，就請他們一起過來吃。）

What better way to send them off?

（還有什麼比用這個方法為他們餞別更好的呢？）

A That's what we thought.

（我們也是這樣想的。）

句型靈活應用

・ **表示你對某事的了解，怎麼說？**

I didn't realize she is 30 years old.

（我不知道她已經 30 歲了。）

I realize you didn't like him very much.

（我知道你不是很喜歡他。）

I realize your mom doesn't want you to stay up.

（我知道你媽媽不喜歡你晚上熬夜。）

・ **問「還有其他更好的方法嗎？」，怎麼說？**

What better way to bring up a child?

（還有比這種更好的方法來教養小孩嗎？）

What better way to say good-bye to them?

（還有比這種更好的方法來向他們道別的嗎？）

What better way to show my appreciation?
（還有比這更好的方法來表示我的感激嗎？）

・說一件即興的事情，怎麼說？

We've had so many impromptu barbecues with them over the years.
（這麼多年來，我們都是臨時決定要烤肉，就請他們過來吃。）

After winning the prize, she gave an impromptu speech.
（在贏得獎牌後，她做了一個即興演說。）

文法句型練習

what 當關係代名詞

＊ 本句型是以 what 當「關係代名詞」，what 所帶出的子句做「主詞補語」。在例句裏就是當 This 和 That 的主詞補語。

▶That's what we thought.
（那就是我們所想的。）

▶This isn't what I ordered.
（這不是我訂的。）

主詞＋ be 動詞＋現在分詞
（要～）

＊ 本句型是以現在進行式，表示已計劃好、將要去做的事。

▶The Smiths are moving next week.
（史密司一家下個禮拜要搬家了。）

▶ We are leaving for USA tomorrow.
（我們明天要前往美國。）

▶ John is going to college this fall.
（約翰這個秋天要上大學。）

談天必用單字

impromptu	[ɪmˈprɑmptju]	即興
barbecue	[ˈbɑrbikju]	烤肉
miss	[mɪs]	懷念
chance	[tʃæns]	機會
appreciation	[əpriʃɪˈeʃən]	感激

談天必用片語

send someone off	為某人餞別
get together	聚在一起

Chapter 7

生活計畫

Unit

29

MP3-30

We're going to the beach.
（我們要去海邊。）

請別人代做事情

Ⓐ Can you cover for me on Sunday?
（這個禮拜天你能幫我代班一下嗎？）
I'm supposed to teach the high school class.
（我原本應該教高中那一班。）

Ⓑ Sure. What's up?
（沒有問題，有事嗎？）

Ⓐ We're going to the beach for the weekend.
（這個周末我們要到海邊去。）

Ⓑ Are you going fishing?
（你要去釣魚嗎？）

Ⓐ No. Just some fun in the sun.
（不，只是在陽光下玩一玩。）
We really need to get away and relax for a few days.
（我們真的需要離開這裏幾天去舒展筋骨。）

Ⓑ Well, don't worry.
（是嘛，不用擔心。）

I'll take care of Sunday school.
（主日學的課我會幫忙照顧。）
You have fun!
（祝你玩得愉快！）

句型靈活應用

- **請別人代班，怎麼說？**

Can you cover for me on Sunday?
（你這個禮拜天能不能幫我代班？）

My colleague agreed to cover for me during my vacation.
（我同事答應在我度假時幫我代班。）

- **問別人有什麼事？**

What's up?
（有什麼事嗎？）

What's the matter?
（有什麼事嗎？）

- **請對方安心**

Well, don't worry.
（是嘛，不要擔心。）

Take it easy.
（安心，慢慢來。）

文法句型練習

Be 動詞＋主詞＋現在分詞？
（要～嗎？）

* 以現在進行式問對方是否要做某事。

▶ **Are you going fishing?**
（你要去釣魚嗎？）

▶ **Are you going to a movie?**
（你要去看電影嗎？）

(You) ＋原形動詞
（你去做～）

* 命令、祈使句中的主詞 You 可以省略掉，但不管 you 有沒有被省略掉，都要用「原形動詞」。

▶ **Have fun.**
（祝你愉快。）

▶ **You have fun.**
（祝你玩得愉快。）

▶ **Have a good trip.**
（祝你旅途愉快。）

▶ **Enjoy yourself.**
（祝你玩得愉快。）

談天必用單字

beach	[bitʃ]	海邊

談天必用片語

cover for someone	幫人代班
take care of	照顧
go fishing	釣魚
get away	離開

Unit

30

MP3-31

Do you want to go see the new movie?
（你要不要去看那部新電影？）

談一部新上映的電影

A There's a new comedy coming out this Friday.
（這個禮拜五有一部新的喜劇要上映。）
Do you want to go see it?
（你要不要去看？）

B What is it about?
（是什麼樣的電影？）

A I'm not real sure.
（我不是很確定。）
I can't remember the actors' names.
（我記不起演員的名字。）
But it has gotten good reviews.
（不過評論不錯。）

B Oh, I know which one you're talking about.
（噢，我知道你在講哪部電影了。）
Where is it playing?
（在哪一家電影院上映？）

A At the theater down the street.
（就在街上那一家戲院。）

B Sounds good.
（好主意。）

I'll talk to you later to finalize things.
（我等一下再和你談，再做決定。）

・ **去做某事，在口語上用 go，後面加原形動詞。**

I'll go see it. （我要去看。）

Go get the paper for me. （去幫我把報紙拿來。）

I'll go find him for you.（我去幫你把他找來。）

・ **講定某事，怎麼說？**

I'll talk to you later to finalize things.
（我等一下再和你談，再做決定。）

We'll finalize the deal over the phone.
（我們在電話裏把交易做最後的決定。）

文法句型練習

> I know which one ＋子句
> （我知道是哪一個。）

＊ 以 which one 帶出來的疑問子句做 "I know" 的受詞。

▶ I know which one you're talking about.
（我知道你在講哪一個。）

▶ I don't know which one he likes better.
（我不知道他比較喜歡哪一個。）

談天必用單字

comedy	[ˈkɑmədɪ]	喜劇
finalize	[ˈfaɪn̩ˌaɪz]	最後決定

Unit

31

MP3-32

I'm busy all next week.
（我下個星期都會很忙。）

久未見面的朋友邀約見面

🅐 We haven't gotten together for a long time.

（我們好久沒有聚在一起了。）

How about lunch later this week?
（這個禮拜稍後我們一起吃個午飯怎麼樣？）

🅑 I don't know.

（我不曉得。）

I'll have to check my schedule.
（我必須查一下我的行程表。）

I'm pretty much tied up all week.
（我這個禮拜時間都很緊。）

🅐 Well, I know I'm busy all next week.

（是嗎，我知道下個禮拜我會很忙。）

I will have a training conference.
（我要參加一個訓練會。）

How about we plan on two weeks from today?
（我們把兩個禮拜後的今天定下來如何？）

B I'm at the corporate offices then.
（那時候我會在總公司。）
But I can make it on that Wednesday.
（不過那個禮拜三還可以。）

A That will work.
（那沒有問題了。）

B O.K.
（好。）
Wednesday in two weeks.
（兩個禮拜後的星期三。）

句型靈活應用

- **時間都排滿了，怎麼說？**

I'm pretty much tied up all week.
（我整個禮拜時間都很緊。）

- **約定時間時，要先看看時間表，怎麼說？**

I don't know. I'll have to check my schedule.
（我不知道，我必須查我的行程表。）

- **事情那樣做成不成？**

That will work.
（那樣做沒有問題。）

That won't work.
（那樣做不行。）

Will that work?
（那樣做可以嗎？）

· **某個時間你有空，怎麼說？**

I can make it on that Wednesday.
（那個星期三我還可以。）

文法句型練習

> 主詞＋現在式動詞＋未來的時間
> （我已經安排好將會～）

＊ 用現在簡單式表示一件你已經安排好，在未來某段時間要做的事。

▶ I'm at the corporate offices then.
（那時候我會在總公司辦公室。）

▶ I'm busy all next week.
（下星期我都會很忙。）

▶ How about we plan on two weeks from today?
（我們把兩周後的今天定下來如何？）

▶ How about going to see a play this weekend?
（我們這個周末去看一場戲如何？）

▶ How about lunch later this week?
（這個禮拜稍後我們一起吃頓午餐如何？）

談天必用單字

training	[ˈtrenɪŋ]	訓練
conference	[ˈkɑnfərəns]	會議

談天必用片語

tie up		纏住

Unit

32

MP3-33

I'm going to New York tomorrow.
（我明天要去紐約。）

談到外地去受訓

A How about going to see a play this weekend?
（這個周末一起去看表演如何？）

B Well, I think I am going to, but I don't think I will be here.
（噢，我是想去，但是我可能不會在這裏。）

A What do you mean?
（什麼意思？）

B I probably won't be in town.
（我也許不在城裏。）

I'm scheduled to go to New York for a training seminar on Thursday.
（我預計這個禮拜四去紐約參加訓練講習會。）

I'm hoping to be able to stay the weekend.
（我一直希望禮拜六還留在那裏。）

I want to see a Broadway show.
（因為我想看一場百老匯的秀。）

A That makes sense.
（那可以理解。）

114

I would certainly prefer to see a Broadway show.
（換成是我，我也想看百老匯的秀。）

B How about catching that play next weekend?
（下個周末再去看表演如何？）

句型靈活應用

- **對方講的話你認為有道理**

  That makes sense.
  （那可以理解。）

  I agree.
  （我同意。）

- **向對方做個提議，怎麼說？**

  How about going to see a play this weekend?
  （這個周末去看場表演如何？）

  How about you?
  （你覺得呢？）

  How about 0a test drive?
  （要不要來試開一下車子？）

談天必用單字

catch	[kætʃ]	趕上
seminar	[ˈsɛməˌnɑr]	講習會

談天必用片語

prefer to		寧願

Unit

33

MP3-34

Where are you going to college?
（你要到哪裏去上大學？）

談上哪一所大學

Ⓐ Where are you going to college?

（你要上哪一所大學？）

Ⓑ I don't know yet.

（我還不知道。）

I've been accepted at Yale, Harvard, Columbia, and Stanford.
（我已被耶魯、哈佛、哥倫比亞和史丹福錄取。）

Ⓐ Wow. Those are all great schools.

（哇，都是好學校耶。）

Ⓑ Yeah, but it really depends on what kind of scholarships I get.

（是的，不過還是要看我得到什麼樣的獎學金來決定。）

I have to go where I can afford to.

（我只能去我付得起的大學。）

A With your grades you should be able to get enough to go wherever

you want.

（以你的成績，你應該拿得到獎學金去任何一所你想要去的大
學。）

B I wish.

（我也這樣希望。）

句型靈活應用

· **對方說的正是你所想要的，但你自己並沒把握，怎麼說？**

I wish.

（我也這樣希望。）

· **對方說一些不太可能實現的願望，你怎麼回答？**

You wish.

（你做夢。）

文法句型練習

> 主詞＋ have ＋ been ＋過去分詞
>   （某人已經被～）

＊ 本句型是現在完成式被動語態，表示某人遭遇的是本身無法操
   控的一件事。

▶ I've been accepted at Yale, Harvard, Columbia, and Stanford.
（我已經被耶魯、哈佛、哥倫比亞和史丹福錄取。）

▶ Three men have been arrested by the police.
（警方已經逮捕了三個人。）

> 子句＋ wherever ＋子句
> （無論任何地方）

＊ wherever 是個關係副詞，指「無論任何地方」。

▶ I wish I could go wherever I want to.
（我希望我能去我想去的地方。）

▶ I'll go wherever you tell me.
（你只要告訴我任何一個地方我都去。）

談天必用單字

scholarship	[ˈskɑlɚʃɪp]	獎學金
grade	[gred]	成績
arrest	[əˈrɛst]	逮捕
afford	[əˈford]	付得起

談天必用片語

| depend on | | 依靠 |
| can afford | | 付得起 |

Chapter 8

娛樂活動

Unit

34

MP3-35

Did you go to watch the fireworks?
（你去看煙火了嗎？）

談看煙火

A Where did you go to watch the fireworks?

（你上哪兒去看煙火表演？）

B We were really lucky.

（我們很幸運。）

There was a country club three blocks from our house.

（離我們家三條街的地方就有一個鄉村俱樂部。）

A You just walked over there?

（你們用走路過去的嗎？）

B No, actually we just sat on the back porch.

（不，事實上，我們只是坐在我們家後門口。）

We could see great from there.

（在那兒我們就看得很清楚了。）

120

A You were lucky.

（你們真幸運。）

We ended up having to fight the crowds at the lake.

（我們最後搞到必須到湖邊，和一大群人擠來擠去。）

B Well, next time give me a call and come over to the house.

（是嗎，下次打個電話到我家裏來。）

It's a whole lot easier.

（那樣子比較容易多了。）

句型靈活應用

- **肯定句在句尾加問號，表示「不確定」。**

You just walk over there?

（你們只用走路過去的嗎？）

- **後來只好做某件事，怎麼說？**

We ended up having to fight the crowds at the lake.

（我們搞到最後必須在湖邊跟一群人擠來擠去。）

We ended up staying home for the holiday.

（我們最後只好在家裏過節。）

＊ 注意 end up 後面要加動名詞。

- **那樣子容易多了，怎麼說？**

It's a whole lot easier.

（那樣會比較容易。）

That would be much easier.
（那樣會容易得多。）

> 命令句 and 命令句
> （做～並做～）

＊ and 連接兩個命令句。因為 and 連接的兩個子句都是命令句，所以兩個子句都把主詞 "You" 省略掉，子句的第一個字是原形動詞。

▶ Give me a call and come over to the house.
（給我個電話，到我家來。）

▶ Give them a call and ask them to help you.
（給他們打電話，叫他們幫你忙。）

談天必用單字

crowd	[kraʊd]	群眾

談天必用片語

come over	到我家來
walk over	步行過去

Unit

35

MP3-36

What did you think about the Christmas parade?

（你認為聖誕節的遊行如何？）

談遊行和花車

A What did your kids think about the Christmas parade?

（你家小孩覺得聖誕遊行如何？）

B They thought it was great.

（他們認為非常好。）

They loved the balloon floats.
（他們最喜歡飄在空中的氣球娃娃。）

A Mine too.

（我也是。）

But Mike liked the bands best.
（可是麥克最喜歡樂隊。）

He always likes the noise.
（他就喜歡那種噪音。）

B Did you see the float with the ski slope?

（你有沒有看見裝成滑雪道的那個花車？）

It really looked like snow.
（上面看起來像真的雪。）

A Yeah, I did.

（是，我看到了。）

I'm not sure what they used.
（我不知道他們用什麼材料。）

Maybe they used snow.
（也許他們就是用雪。）

It was certainly cold enough for it to have stayed frozen.
（那天天氣很冷，雪是不會融化的。）

B I don't think so.

（我想不是雪。）

Because parts of it would melt with the heat from the sun.
（因為雪在太陽的熱度下總有部分會融化。）

A You're probably right.

（也許你是對的！）

句型靈活應用

· **你認為對方可能是對的，怎麼說？**

You're probably right.

（也許你是對的。）

You are quite right.
（你說得真對。）

・**「我的也是一樣」，怎麼說？**

Ⓐ My car needs washing.
（我的車要洗一洗了。）

Ⓑ Mine too.
（我的也是。）

文法句型練習

> 主詞＋動詞＋副詞最高級
> （做得最～）

＊ 動詞需用副詞去修飾，如果要表示「最怎麼樣」時，要用副詞的「最高級」修飾動詞。

▶ John liked the bands best.
（約翰最喜歡樂團。）

▶ Mary runs fastest in her class.
（瑪麗在班上跑得最快。）

談天必用單字

stay frozen		凍而不融
parade	[pə'red]	遊行

melt	[mɛlt]	融化
heat	[hit]	熱
balloon	[bəˈlun]	汽球
float	[flot]	花車
slope	[slop]	斜坡
frozen	[ˈfrozn̩]	冰凍

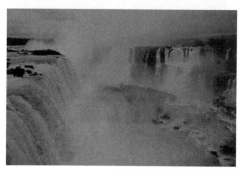

Unit

MP3-37

They are having a huge sale.
（他們有個大拍賣。）

談某商店的大拍賣

A I like your outfit.
（我喜歡你的衣服。）

Is it new?
（是新的嗎？）

B Yes, I got it on sale at the store.
（是的，我在那家店大拍賣時買的。）

They are having a huge sale.
（他們正在舉行大拍賣。）

It was half price.
（這件衣服只有半價。）

A Wow. Did they have a good selection?
（哇，有沒有很多東西可以挑選？）

B Pretty good.
（還可以。）

A lot of the stuff has some little thing wrong.
（有許多東西都有一些小瑕疵。）

A Is that why they are marked down?

（這就是為什麼他們賣得比較便宜嗎？）

B Maybe.

（也許吧。）

句型靈活應用

・ **如何讚美對方**

I like your outfit.

（我喜歡你的打扮。）

I like your hairstyle.

（我喜歡你的髮型。）

・ **有很多東西可以挑選，怎麼說？**

Did they have a good selection?

（他們有很多東西可供挑選嗎？）

They have a wide selection of clothes.

（他們有很多衣服可供挑選。）

文法句型練習

Is that why ＋子句？

（那就是為什麼～的原因嗎？）

* why 是表示問「為什麼」的關係副詞。

▶ Is that why they are marked down?
（那就是為什麼他們賣得比較便宜嗎？）

▶ Is that why you are not allowed to watch TV?
（那就是為什麼你不可以看電視嗎？）

▶ Is that why they didn't attend the meeting?
（那就是為什麼他們沒參加會議的原因嗎？）

談天必用單字

outfit	[ˈaʊtfɪt]	衣著
huge	[hjudʒ]	廣大
selection	[səˈlɛkʃən]	選擇
stuff	[stʌf]	東西
allow	[əˈlaʊ]	允許
attend	[əˈtɛnd]	參加

談天必用片語

on sale	大拍賣
mark down	賣得比較便宜

Unit

37

MP3-38

I went to the ground breaking for the new building.

（我去參加新大樓的破土典禮。）

A Did you go to the ground breaking for the new building?

（你有沒有去參加那棟新大樓的破土典禮？）

B No, I couldn't make it.

（不，我騰不出時間。）

How was it?
（典禮進行得如何？）

A It was real different.

（那整個感覺都不同。）

Not at all what I expected.
（跟我預期的完全不同。）

B How so?

（怎麼會這樣？）

Ⓐ A lot of the people there did not seem to care about the project.

（在那個地方很多人根本不關心這個案子。）

It was just an occasion for a party.
（整個過程只是一個宴會的場合。）

Ⓑ How disappointing!

（多令人失望！）

A lot of people have worked very hard to raise the funds to build the Children's Center.
（很多人花了很大功夫才募集到這筆款子來興建這個兒童中心的。）

句型靈活應用

· **表示某事不如預期，怎麼說？**

Not at all what I expected.

（跟我預期的完全不同。）

Not at all what you thought.

（跟你所想的完全不一樣。）

· **表示不明白為什麼會這樣，怎麼說？**

How so?

（怎麼會這樣呢？）

What happened?

（發生了什麼事？）

- **表示對某事的失望，怎麼說？**

  How disappointing!

  （多令人失望呀！）

> I couldn't ＋原形動詞
>
> （我不能～）

* 表示「我不能做到」，若是過去的事，用 "I couldn't ～ ."，若
  是現在或未來的事，用 "I can not ～ ."；相反地，「我能」用 "I
  could ～ ." 或 "I can ～ ." 來表示。

► I couldn't make it.

   （我沒有辦到。）

► I can make it.

   （我可以辦到。）

ground	[graʊnd]	土地
building	[ˈbɪldɪŋ]	大樓
fund	[fʌnd]	款項
disappoint	[dɪsəˈpɔɪnt]	失望
raise	[rez]	募集

ground breaking		破土

Chapter 9

評論朋友

Unit

38

MP3-39

They are very strict.
（他們很嚴厲。）

談論朋友對小孩子的管教方式

A John and Mary are really strict with their children.

（約翰和瑪麗對小孩的管教很嚴格。）

B What makes you say that?

（你根據什麼這樣說？）

A The kids are not allowed any freedom at all.

（孩子們一點自由都沒有。）

It's like John and Mary want to monitor their every thought.

（就好像約翰和瑪麗要監管小孩的每個思想。）

B Well, they are probably just trying to protect the children.

（是嗎，也許他們只是想保護小孩吧。）

Ⓐ Maybe, but it seems like all they are doing is controlling them.

（也許，但似乎他們所做的只是想控制小孩。）

The kids don't really know how to make choices.

（孩子們都不知道應該怎樣來做選擇了。）

Ⓑ Well, one day the kids will figure out they don't have to report their every move.

（是嗎，總有一天孩子們會知道他們不需要每個動作都要跟父母報告。）

And then there will be a major rebellion.

（到那時候可就有一場大革命了。）

句型靈活應用

・ 說某件事好像如何，怎麼說？

It's like they want to monitor their every thought.

（那好像他們要監管他們的每個思想。）

It seems like they are not happy.

（看起來他們好像並不快樂。）

文法句型練習

主詞＋ be 動詞＋過去分詞

＊ 本句型是「被動語態」，以下的例句都是否定句，所以在 be 動詞後面加 not。

▶ The kids are not allowed any freedom at all.
（小孩子連一點點自由都得不到允許。）

▶ We are not allowed to go out at night.
（我們晚上不准出去。）

談天必用單字

strict	[strɪkt]	嚴格
freedom	[ˈfridəm]	自由
monitor	[ˈmɑnətɚ]	監視
control	[kənˈtrol]	控制
report	[rɪˈpɔrt]	報告
rebellion	[rɪˈbɛljən]	反叛
allow	[əˈlaʊ]	允許
protect	[prəˈtɛkt]	保護
move	[muv]	行動

談天必用片語

not at all		一點也不

Unit

MP3-40

He's got a great sense of humor.

（他很有幽默感。）

談一個很幽默的朋友

A I really like Mike.

（我真的很喜歡麥克。）

He always makes me laugh.

（他總是讓我發笑。）

B You're right.

（你說得對。）

He's got a great sense of humor.

（他很有幽默感。）

A Somehow he is able to help me laugh about stuff that is really quite painful.

（即使是非常痛苦的事，他還是有辦法逗我笑。）

B I know what you mean.

（我知道你的意思。）

He understands how healing humor can be.
（他知道幽默感多麼具有醫療效用。）

A Yes, and he can help people feel better.
（是的，他可以使人們覺得舒服一點。）

句型靈活應用

- **說某人有幽默感，怎麼說？**

  He's got a great sense of humor.
  （他很有幽默感。）

文法句型練習

主詞＋ make ＋受詞＋原形動詞
（令人～）

* make 和 help 都是使役動詞，受詞之後的動詞要用原形動詞。

▶He always makes me laugh.
（他總是讓我笑。）

▶They made him lose his patience.
（他們讓他失去耐心。）

▶He can help people feel better.
（他可以讓人們覺得舒服一點。）

子句＋ how ＋形容詞＋子句
（多麼地～）

* how 是「多麼地」的意思，how+ 形容詞所帶出的子句做 understand 和 know 的受詞。

▶ He understands how healing humor can be.
（他知道幽默感很具醫療效果。）

▶ Do you understand how healing laughter can be?
（你知道笑有多富醫療效用嗎？）

▶ I know how important water is.
（我知道水是多麼重要。）

談天必用單字

sense	[sɛns]	感官
humor	[ˈhjumɚ]	幽默
painful	[ˈpenfḷ]	痛苦
healing	[ˈhilɪŋ]	醫療效用
laughter	[ˈlæftɚ]	笑

Unit

40

MP3-41

I think John is mean.
（我認為約翰很差勁。）

談一位差勁的朋友

A I don't know what's wrong with John.
（我不知道約翰是怎麼了。）

I'm beginning to think he's just plain mean!
（我開始覺得他很差勁。）

B What do you mean?
（你這話什麼意思？）

A Well, Tom asked Peter, John's son, if he would like to come over and play some games on the computer.
（噢，湯姆邀請約翰的兒子彼得到我們家來玩電腦遊戲。）

John told Tom that Peter wasn't allowed to play with him anymore.
（約翰對湯姆說，彼得不可以再和他玩。）

B What on earth for?
（那到底為了什麼？）

140

A That's what the boys asked.

（那也是小孩們問的問題。）

Apparently it was news to Tom also.
（很顯然地，這對湯姆來說也是新聞。）

B That's not just mean.

（那不叫做差勁。）

It's demented!
（那簡直叫做發瘋。）

句型靈活應用

- **在有 what, who, when 等的疑問句，加強語氣的說法，怎麼用？**

What on earth for?

（到底是為什麼？）

What on earth do you mean?

（你到底是什麼意思？）

Who on earth do you think you are?

（你以為你是誰？）

When on earth do you expect me to do this?

（你到底要我怎麼做？）

- **表示對某事完全不知情，怎麼說？**

It was news to John.

（這對約翰來說是個大新聞。）

It was a new one on me.

（這對我來説是個新消息。）

文法句型練習

what 做關係代名詞

* what 做「關係代名詞」，所帶出的子句可以做「主詞補語」。
在以下的例句中就是做 that 的主詞補語。

▶ That's what the boys asked.

（那是孩子們要問的問題。）

▶ That's what I wanted to know.

（那是我想知道的。）

談天必用單字

apparently	[ə'pærəntlɪ]	明顯的
plain	[plen]	平凡
mean	[min]	卑鄙
demented	[di'mɛntɪd]	發狂
expect	[ɪks'pɛkt]	預期

Unit

She is so down to earth.
（她很平易近人。）

談一位平易近人的朋友

A Mary is so down to earth.

（瑪麗真是平易近人。）

B I know what you mean.

（我知道你的意思。）

A It is so nice to be with her.

（和她在一起實在很好。）

B You're right.

（一點都沒錯。）

A Did you know that she fixed dinner for my family every night the first week I went back to work?

（你知道我又回去上班的第一週，她每晚都來為我家人做晚飯嗎？）

B That's incredible.
（真難相信。）

Most people wouldn't even think about
something like that, let alone do it.
（大部分人連想都想不到，更何況幫你忙。）

句型靈活應用

・ **你覺得某事很不可思議，怎麼說？**

That's incredible.
（真難相信。）

・ **強調「沒有」，怎麼說？**

I don't have a dime, let alone a dollar.
（我連一毛錢都沒有，更別說一塊錢了。）

I didn't hear his name, let alone know him.
（我連他的名字都沒聽過，更何況是認識他。）

文法句型練習

It is so + nice +不定詞
（～是多麼好。）

＊ It 是「虛主詞」，真正的主詞是後面的不定詞，It is so nice to
be with her. 就是 To be with her is so nice. 的意思。

▶ It is so nice to be with her.
（跟她在一起實在很好。）

▶ It is so nice to work with him.
（跟他一起工作實在很好。）

▶ It is nice to meet you.
（見到你實在很高興。）

談天必用單字

incredible	[ɪnˈkrɛdəb!]	難以相信
fix	[fɪks]	做
dime	[daɪm]	一角錢

談天必用片語

down to earth	平易近人
think about	想到
let alone	何況
fix dinner	做晚飯

Chapter 10

發表意見

Unit

42

MP3-43

What did you think about that book?
（你認為那本書怎麼樣？）

談一本書

A What did you think about that book?

（你認為那本書怎麼樣？）

B I'm not real sure.

（我不是很確定。）

Some of it was O.K..
（裏面的某些部分還好。）

A I know what you mean.

（我知道你的意思。）

He kind of got off track in the middle section.
（他到了中間那部分，主題就偏了。）

B That's what is was.

（真的就是這樣。）

Let me put it this way.
（讓我這樣説好了，）

I know I won't reread it.
（我知道我不會再重看一次。）

And I wouldn't recommend it to anyone, either.
（而且，我也不會把它推薦給任何人。）

句型靈活應用

・ 表示不確定，怎麼說？

I'm not real sure.

（我不是很確定。）

・ 表示對某事的看法，怎麼說？

It's great.

（那太好了。）

It's O.K.

（那還好。）

It's pretty bad.

（那真的很糟。）

・ 長話短說如何起頭？

Let me put it this way.

（讓我這樣說好了。）

文法句型練習

kind of something

（有點～）

* kind of 是副詞，是一句口語，表示「有點～」的意思。

▶ He kind of got off track in the middle section.
（他到了中間那一部分，就偏離主題。）

▶ That was kind of a stupid thing to do.
（做那種事真的有一點傻。）

▶ I kind of like him.
（我有一點喜歡他。）

談天必用單字

track	[træk]	路徑
section	[ˈsɛkʃən]	部分
recommend	[ˌrɛkəˈmɛnd]	推薦

談天必用片語

get off track	偏離主題

Unit

43

MP3-44

What is your favorite place?

（你最喜歡的地方是哪裏？）

討論要去哪裏吃飯

Ⓐ Where do you feel like going for dinner?

（你想去哪兒吃晚飯？）

Ⓑ What I really like is some good Chinese food.

（我只是想吃頓中國菜。）

Ⓐ That sounds good.

（好主意。）

Ⓑ What is your favorite place?

（你最喜歡哪一家？）

Ⓐ There's a little restaurant on the corner.

（轉角那個地方有一家小餐館。）

I'm not even sure it has a name.
（我甚至連名字都不知道。）

Ⓑ Sounds good.

（聽起來不錯。）

Let's go there.
（我們就去那裏吧。）

· 問對方的意見

Where do you feel like going for dinner?
（你想到哪裏去吃晚飯？）

What movie do you feel like seeing?
（你想看哪部電影？）

文法句型練習

what 當關係代名詞

* what 當關係代名詞所帶出的子句可以當整個句子的「主詞」。

▶ What I really like is some good Chinese food.
（我真的想做的，是吃一頓好的中國菜。）

▶ What I really care is his grade.
（我真的在意的，是他的成績。）

談天必用單字

favorite	[ˈfevərɪt]	最喜歡的
corner	[ˈkɔrnɚ]	角落
grade	[gred]	成績

談天必用片語

feel like		想要

Unit

44

MP3-45

Opera isn't real appealing to me.

（歌劇並不是真的很吸引我。）

去聽歌劇

A I have a pair of tickets to the opera Saturday night.

（我有兩張禮拜六晚上的歌劇票。）

Would you like to go?

（你要不要去看？）

B I don't think so.

（我不想去。）

I'm not too wild about opera.

（我對歌劇不是很熱衷。）

A What do you not like?

（你不喜歡哪一點？）

B Well, it's just not my thing.

（噢，那就不是我喜歡的東西。）

People singing in Italian just isn't real

Chapter 10 發表意見

appealing to me.

（聽人家用義大利文唱歌，實在對我沒有什麼吸引力。）

A It's not like that at all.

（事情根本不像你所說的。）

This particular opera is in English.
（我說的這部歌劇是英語發音。）

Have you ever been to the opera?
（你有沒有看過歌劇？）

B Actually, no.

（實際上，沒有。）

If it's in English, maybe I should give it a try.
（它要是用英語的話，也許我還可以去試一試。）

句型靈活應用

· **表示某事或某人不適合你，怎麼說？**

It's just not my thing.

（那根本不合我的胃口。）

He's just not your type.

（他根本不適合你。）

· **表示某事並不吸引你，怎麼說？**

Opera is not appealing to me.

（歌劇對我沒有吸引力。）

It's not a movie appealing to anyone.

（那部電影不是對每個人都有吸引力。）

- 對方的想法並不正確，你怎麼說？

  It's not like that at all.

  （事情根本不如你所想像的。）

- 「使用」某種語言，英文介系詞用 in

  The novel is written in Chinese.

  （這本小說是用中文寫的。）

  The opera is in English.

  （這部歌劇是用英語發音。）

- 表示願意嘗試，怎麼說？

  Maybe I should give it a try.

  （也許我應該試試看。）

文法句型練習

> Have + you + ever been ～ ?
>
> （你曾經去過～嗎？）

＊ 本句型是用現在完成式的句型，問對方是否曾經去過某地。

▶ Have you ever been to the opera?

（你有沒有看過歌劇？）

▶ Have you ever been abroad?

（你有沒有到過國外？）

▶ Have you ever been to Europe?

（你有沒有到過歐洲？）

opera	[ˈɑpərə]	歌劇
appeal	[əˈpil]	吸引
particular	[pɚˈtɪkjəlɚ]	特別
abroad	[əˈbrod]	國外
actually	[ˈæktʃʊəlɪ]	事實上

談天必用片語

not at all	一點也不
appealing to	對某人有吸引力

Unit

I'm crazy about jazz.

（我對爵士樂很著迷。）

談爵士樂

A Do you like jazz?
（你喜歡爵士樂嗎？）

B I love it!
（我喜歡透了。）
How about you?
（你呢？）

A I'm crazy about it.
（我對爵士樂很著迷。）

B Have you heard that new trio that's playing at the Jazz Club?
（你聽過正在爵士俱樂部裏演唱的新三人組嗎？）

A No, I haven't.
（不，還沒有。）
I've heard that they are really good.
（不過我聽說他們唱得非常棒。）

B Actually, I think they are fantastic!
（事實上，我認為他們太好了。）

· 表示著迷、熱衷，怎麼說？

I'm crazy about jazz.
（我對爵士樂非常著迷。）

I'm not too crazy about basketball.
（我對籃球不是很熱衷。）

I'm not too wild about jazz.
（我對爵士樂不很熱衷。）

文法句型練習

> that 當關係代名詞

* 下列句型中，that 當關係代名詞，所代替的名詞是「正在上演的電影、
  比賽或表演」。因為強調「正在進行」，所以用 "that's playing"。

▶ I'm going to see the show that's playing at the Fine Art Center.
（我要去看表演藝術中心的表演。）

▶ We're going to see the basketball game that's playing at the stadium.
（我們要去看正在體育館開打的籃球賽。）

▶ Have you heard that new trio that's playing at the Jazz Club?
（你聽過在爵士俱樂部演唱的新三人組沒有？）

談天必用單字

fantastic	[fənˈtæstɪk]	太好了
trio	[ˈtrɪo]	三人組
stadium	[ˈstedɪəm]	球場
jazz	[dʒæz]	爵士樂

Unit

MP3-47

Their pastries are to die for!

（他們的糕餅好吃得不得了！）

談附近新開的麵包店

A Have you been to the new bakery on the corner?
（你有沒有去過轉角那家新開的麵包店？）

B No, how is it?
（沒有，那家店怎麼樣？）

A It is heaven!
（那簡直是天堂！）
Their pastries are to die for!
（他們的糕點好吃得不得了！）

B Really? How is their bread?
（真的嗎？他們的麵包呢？）

A It's really good, too.
（也很好。）

B Is it better than the bread from the bakery down
the street?
（比街上那一邊麵包店的麵包還要好嗎？）

A I think so.
（我想是的。）

・ 表示某件東西非常好，怎麼說？

Their music are to die for!
（他們的音樂好聽得不得了！）

Their food are to die for!
（他們的食物好吃得不得了！）

文法句型練習

> S from A 地 is better than that from B 地
> （A 地的 S 比 B 地的更好。）

* 本句的比較句型是比較從兩個不同地方來的東西，所以 than 後面加 that，這個 that 是代名詞，代替從 A 地來的東西，例如以下例句中的 bread。

▶ **The bread from Katy's bakery is better than that from Garden's.**
（凱蒂麵包店的麵包比佳頓的還要好吃。）

▶ **Is the bread from Katy's bakery better than that from Garden's?**
（凱蒂麵包店的麵包比佳頓的還要好吃嗎？）

談天必用單字

pastry	[ˈpæstrɪ]	糕點

談天必用片語

die for	好得不得了

Chapter 11

遇到麻煩

Unit

47

MP3-48

You look really stressed out.
（你看起來壓力很大。）

談工作上的困擾

A What's wrong?

（怎麼了？）

You look really stressed out.
（你看起來好像壓力很大。）

B I am. I have to meet a deadline for this report.

（我是壓力很大，這篇報告必須趕上截止日期。）

And I'm still waiting on some figures from Jane.
（可是我還在等珍妮給我一些數字。）

A Does she have them?

（她的數字弄好了嗎？）

B Not even close.

（還早得很啦。）

She went on vacation last week and hasn't

even started.

（她上個禮拜去度假，到現在都還沒開始弄呢。）

A Can you put the report together and then add an appendix with

her figures in it?

（你能不能先把報告做完，然後加上一個附錄，把她的數字再擺進去？）

B That's a good idea.

（那是個好主意。）

Then if she doesn't get it done, it's her fault, not mine.

（那樣一來，她沒做好是她的錯，不是我的錯。）

句型靈活應用

・ **對方受到很大的壓力，你怎麼說？**

You look really stressed out.

（你看起來好像壓力很大。）

・ **認為對方的建議很好，怎麼說？**

That's a good idea.

（那是個好主意。）

文法句型練習

mine 是我的某某東西

＊ mine 在中文翻譯成「我的」，實際上，mine 是「我的某某東西」，

這裡的「某某東西」要視句意來決定。下面句中第一句的 mine 指 my fault，第二句的 mine 是 my book。

▶ It's her fault, not mine.
（那是她的錯，不是我的錯。）

▶ It's Mary's book, not mine.
（那是瑪麗的書，不是我的。）

談天必用單字

stress	[strɛs]	壓力
deadline	[ˈdɛdlaɪn]	截止日期
figure	[ˈfɪgjɚ]	數字
fault	[fɔlt]	錯誤
appendix	[əˈpɛndɪks]	附錄

談天必用片語

stress out	壓力很大
wait on	等候
go on vacation	度假
put them together	把它們做好

Unit

MP3-49

I don't have the foggiest idea.

（我一點都不知道。）

談工作上算出的金額不相符

🅐 I can't seem to get these figures to come out right.

（我一直沒有辦法把這些數字湊回正確數目。）

🅑 What are they supposed to be?

（正確的數目應該是什麼？）

🅐 Home office is showing our overhead costs to be $850,000 a month.

（總公司顯示我們的固定成本是一個月 85 萬。）

I don't have the foggiest idea where they are getting that number from.

（我就不知道他們是去哪裏去拿到那個數字。）

🅑 Do you think that maybe they made the error?

（你認為他們可能犯錯嗎？）

A Yes, but I can't seem to convince them of that.

（是的，可是我就是不能說服他們。）

I'm only coming up with $610,000.

（我的數字只達到 61 萬。）

I sure would like to know where the other $240,000 is coming from.

（我一直都想知道多餘的 24 萬是從哪裏來的。）

B Why don't you call them and have them walk you through their figures?

（你為什麼不打電話給他們，讓他們把他們的數字一筆筆和你的核對一次？）

· 強調你不知道，怎麼說？

I don't have the foggiest idea.

（我一點都不知道。）

· 說服別人怎麼說？

I convince them of my point.

（我說服他們相信我的決定。）

I can't convince her of the need to study.

（我不能讓她相信讀書是必須的。）

· 問某件事「應該如何」，怎麼說？

What are they supposed to be?

（他們應該是怎麼樣？）

It's supposed to snow today.

（今天應該會下雪。）

They are supposed to get here any minute now.

（他們隨時都有可能抵達。）

· 帶著某人一起看一件問題，怎麼說？

Do they walk you through their figures?

（他們把他們的數字一筆筆和你們核對過嗎？）

Do I have to walk you through this solution?

（我須要把這個解決辦法一步步做給你看嗎？）

文法句型練習

> Why don't you ～ ?
>
> （你為何不～？）

▶ Why don't you have them walk you through their figures?

（你為什麼不叫他們把他們的數字一條條和你核對一下呢？）

▶ Why don't you have her do the dishes for you?

（你為什麼不讓她幫你洗碗？）

談天必用單字

come up with		想出
overhead	['ovɚ͵hɛd]	固定成本
error	['ɛrɚ]	錯誤

Unit
49

MP3-50

What happened?
（發生了什麼事？）

談如何把地毯上的酒漬清除掉

A What are you doing?
（你在幹嘛？）

B Trying to get this wine stain out of the carpet.
（我試著要把毯子上的這個酒漬去掉。）

A What happened?
（發生什麼事了？）

B I hit Mary and knocked her wine glass out of her hand.
（我撞到瑪麗，把她手上的酒杯撞掉了。）

A Hang on.
（等一下。）

There's some soda in here.
（這裡有些小蘇打。）

It should take the stain right out.
（它應該可以把那些痕跡去掉。）

B Really?

（真的嗎？）

That's a new one on me.
（這對我還算是新聞。）

Hey, it really is working.
（嗨，真的有效耶。）

句型靈活應用

・ **請別人稍待，怎麼說？**

Hang on.

（等一下。）

・ **表示有效或無效，怎麼說？**

It really is working.

（真的有效耶。）

It won't work.

（毫無效果。）

談天必用單字

carpet	[ˈkɑrpɪt]	地毯
stain	[sten]	痕跡
knock	[nɑk]	敲
glass	[glæs]	玻璃杯

Unit

50

MP3-51

What's up?
（有什麼事？）

印表機的紙卡住了

A You look like you're having trouble.

（你看起來好像有困難。）

What's up?
（怎麼啦？）

B This stupid printer.

（這個笨印表機。）

I can't get these documents printed.
（我就是不能把這些文件印出來。）

The paper keeps jamming.
（它一直在卡紙。）

A I hate it when it does that.

（我最討厭卡紙了。）

B I know there's a trick to it

（我知道有個辦法可以解決。）

I don't remember what it is.
（但我記不起來是什麼辦法。）

A I don't know.

（我不知道。）

But sometimes I just turn it off
（有時候我只是把它關掉。）

Then I turn it on again and it's fixed.
（然後再把它打開，它就好了。）

B That's it. Thanks.

（果然有效，謝謝。）

I knew it was something really simple.
（我知道解決的方法一定很簡單。）

句型靈活應用

・ 表示某事一直發生，怎麼說？

The paper keeps jamming.

（一直在卡紙。）

The phone keeps ringing.

（電話一直在響。）

・ 說做某事的技巧，怎麼說？

I know there's a trick to it.

（我知道有一個辦法可以解決。）

He knows the tricks to fix the TV.

（他知道一個高招可以把電視修好。）

> get ＋受詞＋過去分詞

* get 是「使役動詞」，使役動詞後面的受詞如果是「事物」時，因為事物不會自己做動作，所以接下去的動詞要用過去分詞，表示被動。

▶ I can't get these documents printed.
（我沒有辦法印出這些文件。）

▶ I can't get the car started.
（我沒辦法發動這部車子。）

談天必用單字

document	[ˈdɑkjəmənt]	文件
printer	[ˈprɪntɚ]	印表機
jam	[dʒæm]	卡紙
trick	[trɪk]	詭計
fix	[fɪks]	修理

談天必用片語

turn on	打開
turn off	關掉

Unit

51

MP3-52

What did you do?

（你做了什麼事？）

時間上忙不過來

A I don't believe I did this.

（我真不敢相信我會這樣做。）

B What did you do?

（你做了什麼？）

A My schedule this afternoon is an absolute mess.

（我今天下午的行程完全亂了。）

Between 3:00 and 3:30 I am supposed to be in four different places.

（3 點到 3 點半之間我要同時出現在四個不同的地方。）

There's no way.

（那根本是不可能的事。）

B I've done that before.

（我以前也出過這樣的問題。）

Anything I can help you with?
（有什麼事是我可以幫忙的嗎？）

· **告訴對方這種事你以前也做過，怎麼說？**

I've done that before.

（我以前也這樣做過。）

· **向對方提議要幫忙，怎麼說？**

Anything I can help you with?

（有什麼事我可以幫忙的？）

文法句型練習

I don't believe ＋子句
（我不相信～）

＊ I don't believe 後面所接的子句，就是「我不相信的事情」。

▶ I don't believe I did this.
（我不相信我會這麼做。）

▶ I don't believe it's snowing in the summer.
（我不相信在夏天竟然會下起雪來。）

談天必用單字

schedule	[ˈskɛdʒul]	行程
absolute	[ˈæbsəlut]	絕對

Chapter 12

談心閒聊

Unit

52

MP3-53

Do you play the lottery?

（你買彩券嗎？）

談彩券

A Do you play the lottery?

（你玩彩券嗎？）

B Every now and then.

（偶爾。）

My kids like to pick the numbers.
（我的小孩喜歡選號碼。）

A Mine like to get the scratch-off tickets.

（我的小孩喜歡玩「刮刮樂」。）

B So do mine.

（我的小孩也喜歡。）

When they win a couple of bucks, we all go
get some ice cream.
（他們贏到幾塊錢的時候，我們就去吃冰淇淋。）

A What a great idea!

（那真是好主意。）

B Well, it teaches them it's really just a game.

（是嘛，那是教他們玩彩券只是個遊戲。）

句型靈活應用

· **表示對方的主意很好，怎麼說？**

What a great idea!

（那是個好主意。）

It's a great idea.

（那是個好主意。）

文法句型練習

> Mine=My ＋名詞
> （我的某某東西）

* Mine 就是 my「我的」再加上前面提過的東西。口語上為了求簡單，就用 mine 一個字來代替。

▶ **A** My teachers like to have pop quizzes.

（我的老師喜歡隨堂測驗。）

▶ **B** So do mine.

（我的老師也是。）

▶ **A** My kids like to play the video games.

（我的小孩喜歡玩電動玩具。）

► **B** Mine don't really like them.

（我的小孩不太喜歡。）

lottery	[ˈlɑtərɪ]	彩券
scratch	[skrætʃ]	刮
buck	[bʌk]	元（錢的單位）

every now and then	偶爾
scratch off	刮開
a couple of	一、兩個

Unit

Have you seen the new play?

（你看過那部新的話劇嗎？）

談新上演的話劇

A Have you seen the new play at Main Street Theater?

（你看過主街戲院新上演的那部話劇嗎？）

B No, but it got great reviews in the paper.

（沒有，不過報上給的評論很好。）

A Yes, I saw those.

（是啊，我看過那些評論。）

I'm hoping to go next Saturday.
（我正希望下個禮拜六能去看。）

B Do you have tickets?

（你有票嗎？）

A No, I am going to call about them tomorrow.

（沒有，我打算明天打個電話去問。）

B Well, believe it or not , the play is actually sold out for the next month!

（這樣子呀，相不相信，到下個月的票都已經賣完了。）

句型靈活應用

・ 說電影得到佳評，怎麼說？

The movie got great reviews in the paper.

（報上給這部電影的評論很好。）

談天必用單字

| review | [rɪ'vju] | 評論 |

談天必用片語

call about	打電話詢問
believe it or not	信不信由你
sold out	售完

Unit

MP3-55

What did you think?

（你認為怎麼樣？）

談學校的新校長

🅐 Have you met the new school principal?

（你和新校長會過面了嗎？）

🅑 Not yet. How about you?

（還沒有，你呢？）

🅐 Yes, I had a chance to talk with her last week.

（我見過了。上個禮拜有個機會和她談過話。）

🅑 Oh really, what did you think?

（噢，真的，你對她看法如何？）

🅐 She was very nice.

（她人很好。）

🅑 That's great.

（那太好了。）

- **問對方的意見，怎麼說？**

What did you think?

（你認為如何？）

談天必用單字

principal	[ˈprɪnsəpl̩]	校長
chance	[tʃæns]	機會

談天必用片語

talk with	與某人談話

Unit

MP3-56

Boy, are the lines long today!

（哇塞，今天的隊伍好長啊！）

超市裏結帳處大排長龍

A Boy, are the lines long today!

（哇塞，今天排得這麼長。）

B I don't understand why they never have enough checkers in the late afternoon.

（我就不知道他們為什麼在黃昏這段時間的櫃台老是開得不夠多。）

A You would think the managers would realize that people stop at the grocery on their way home from work.

（我們總以為經理應該了解客人下班回家途中會來店裏買東西。）

B You're right.

（你説得對。）

A Why don't they open more lanes?

（他們為什麼就不會多開幾條線？）

B Wait, it looks like they are finally opening one more.

（等等，看起來好像他們終於要多開一條線啦。）

Yes, they are!

（沒錯，他們正要多開一線。）

句型靈活應用

• 「往某地的路上」，怎麼說？

I'm on my way home from work.

（我正好在下班回家的途中。）

I met Mary on my way to work.

（我在上班途中遇到瑪麗。）

談天必用單字

checker	['tʃɛkɚ]	收銀台
lane	[len]	小道
manager	['mænɪdʒɚ]	經理

談天必用片語

look like		好像

Chapter 13

上班族交談

Unit

56

MP3-57

I'm going to apply for that position.
（我要去應徵那個職位。）

談應徵助理主計員

🅰 Are you going to apply for the new assistant controller's position?

（你要不要去申請那個新的助理主計的位子？）

🅱 I haven't decided yet.

（我還沒有決定。）

🅰 Why not?

（為什麼沒有？）

You are certainly the most qualified.
（你肯定是最有資格的。）

🅱 It's not that I can't do the work. I can.

（不是說我不能勝任，我當然可以。）

But I don't know if all the overtime that's required is worth it.
（但那個職位要求很多加班，我不知道這樣做是不是值得。）

Ⓐ Are you kidding?

（你在開什麼玩笑？）

Ⓑ No, I have other things to do other than just
work.

（不，是真的。除了上班，我總得做點其他的事呀！）

句型靈活應用

· 對方說的話你不相信，怎麼說？

Are you kidding?

（你在開玩笑？）

· 表示你不只是這件事要做，怎麼說？

I have other things to do other than just work.

（除了工作，我總得做點其他的事。）

文法句型練習

> the most ＋過去分詞
> （最～的）

＊ 本句型用過去分詞當形容詞，most 是表示形容詞「最」的意思。

▶ You are the most qualified.

（你是最有資格的。）

▶ She is the most talented.

（她是最有天分的。）

＊ 本句型有一個由關係代名詞that所組成的子句在特別說明主詞。

▶ All the overtime that's required is not worth it.
（這些必須的加班都是不值得的。）

▶ All the money that we've raised was wasted.
（我們募來的所有的錢都浪費掉了。）

談天必用單字

assistant	[əˈsɪstənt]	助理
controller	[kənˈtrolɚ]	主計員
position	[pəˈzɪʃən]	職位
qualified	[ˈkwɑlɪfaɪd]	資格

談天必用片語

apply for		申請

Unit

57

MP3-58

They fired John.
（他們把約翰辭掉。）

談被裁員的同事

Ⓐ Did you hear about John?
（你聽說約翰的事嗎？）

Ⓑ No, what happened?
（沒有，怎麼了？）

Ⓐ They let him go.
（他們把他辭掉了。）

Ⓑ You mean they fired him?
（你的意思是他們開除他了？）
When?
（什麼時候？）

Ⓐ Apparently last night.
（很顯然是昨天晚上。）
The auditors found a bunch of inconsistencies

in the books.

（稽核部門發現帳目有許多不清楚的地方。）

And they were all directly traceable to John.

（每一個不清楚的地方都可直接追溯到約翰。）

B I'm shocked.

（我覺得好驚訝。）

Who would ever expect John to be cheating?

（誰會想到約翰竟然會詐欺？）

句型靈活應用

・ **問對方有沒有聽說某事，怎麼說？**

Did you hear about John?

（你有沒有聽說約翰的事？）

Did you hear about the rumor?

（你有沒有聽說過這個謠言？）

・ **在肯定句句尾加問號，表示不確定的用法**

You mean they fired him?

（你指他們開除了他？）

文法句型練習

主詞＋be 動詞＋過去分詞

（某人很～）

＊ 表示「使人感到某種情緒」的動詞，例如：shock, excite 和

frighten，要用過去分詞。

▶ I'm shocked.
（我很震驚。）

▶ I'm excited.
（我很興奮。）

▶ I'm frightened.
（我很害怕。）

談天必用單字

traceable	[ˈtresəbl]	可追溯的
inconsistency	[ˌɪnkənˈsɪstənsɪ]	前後不相符
shocked	[ʃɑkt]	震驚
auditor	[ˈɔdɪtɚ]	稽查員
bunch	[bʌntʃ]	一束
rumor	[ˈrumɚ]	謠言
excited	[ɪkˈsaɪtɪd]	興奮的
frightened	[ˈfraɪtn̩d]	害怕的

談天必用片語

a bunch of		很多

Unit

58

MP3-59

Have you heard the latest news about the takeover?
（你有沒有聽到有關併購的最新消息？）

談公司併購

🅐 Have you heard the latest news about the takeover?

（你有沒有聽說有關被接管的最新消息？）

🅑 Well, I don't think it's exactly a takeover, more a merger.

（噢，我不認為那是接管，應該比較像是併購。）

🅐 What's the difference?

（有什麼不同？）

Someone else is going to own the company and be running it.

（公司就要被別人擁有，被別人經營了。）

🅑 Not necessarily.

（也不是全然如此。）

From what I understand the management is going to stay the same.
（據我了解，所有的主管都會留任。）

And there are no areas of duplication.
（況且並沒有營業範圍的重複。）

So everyone's job is pretty safe.
（所以每個人的職位應該都很安全。）

A Really?
（真的嗎？）

I heard that they were just buying out the company to sell it off piece by piece.
（我聽說他們只是把公司買下來，然後把公司分割成一部分一部分賣掉。）

B No.
（不會的。）

句型靈活應用

・ **聽到一些消息，怎麼說？**

Have you heard the latest news about the takeover?
（你有沒有聽說被接管的最新消息？）

I heard that you bought a new house.
（我聽說你買了新房子。）

> From what I understand ＋子句
> （就我所了解的～）

＊ From what I understand 後面的子句就是指「我所了解的事情」。

▶ **From what I understand the management is going to stay the same.**
（根據我的了解，所有的主管都會留任。）

▶ **From what I understand he is not going to be the new CEO.**
（根據我的了解，他不會擔任新的總經理。）

談天必用單字

takeover	[ˈtekˈovɚ]	接管
merger	[ˈmɝdʒɚ]	合併
duplication	[djuplɪˈkeʃən]	重複
necessarily	[ˈnɛsəsɛrɪlɪ]	必然地

談天必用片語

buy out	**全數購買**
sell off	分售
piece by piece	一部分、一部分地

Chapter 14

度假旅遊

Unit

59

MP3-60

Where do you want to go on vacation this year?

（你今年要去哪裏度假？）

談度假計劃

A Where do you want to go on vacation this year?
（你今年要到哪裏去度假？）

B Somewhere sunny and relaxing, but not too hot.
（有陽光、可以放輕鬆的地方，但不要太熱。）

A How about somewhere in Southern Taiwan?
（在南台灣找個地方怎麼樣？）

B That sounds good.
（聽起來不錯。）

Maybe Ken-Ding National Park or some place quiet.
（也許墾丁公園或其他比較安靜的地方。）

Ⓐ Maybe, what about a cruise?

（也許吧，來個「船之旅」如何？）

Ⓑ No, ships tend to be pretty crowded.

（不，坐船一般都比較擁擠。）

I really want to be alone some.
（我真的希望人能比較少一點。）

Ⓐ Okay, let's see what the travel agent can find in Southern Taiwan.

（好吧，那就讓我們看看，旅行社能幫我們在南台灣找到什麼地方。）

句型靈活應用

· 表示人或事比較有某種傾向，怎麼說？

Ships tend to be pretty crowded.

（搭船一般都比較擁擠。）

John tends to be lazy.

（約翰比較懶一些。）

Does the island tends to be hot in the summer?

（這個島在夏天會比較熱嗎？）

文法句型練習

Let's see ＋疑問子句
（讓我們來看看～）

* what 所帶出來的疑問子句就是「我們要來看看」的事情，也就是當 Let's see 的受詞。

▶ **Let's see what the travel agent can find in Southern Taiwan.**
（讓我們看看旅行社能幫我們在南台灣找到什麼地方。）

▶ **Let's see what I can do.**
（讓我們看看我能做到什麼程度。）

▶ **Let's see what they have to say.**
（讓我們看看他們到底要講什麼話。）

談天必用單字

sunny	[ˈsʌnɪ]	陽光的
relaxing	[rɪˈlæksɪŋ]	放輕鬆的
alone	[aˈlon]	單獨
agent	[ˈedʒənt]	代理人

談天必用片語

go on vacation	去度假

Unit

How was your vacation?
（你的假期如何？）

談假期

A How was your vacation?
（你的假期過得如何？）

B It was great.
（非常好。）
All I did was play and rest and have a ton of fun.
（我整個假期做的就是玩、休息，一大堆樂趣。）

A Where all did you go?
（你都去什麼地方？）

B We went to the coast to see my sister for a few days.
（我們到沿海去看我姐姐幾天。）
And then flew down to Mexico City and then stopped in San Antonio for a few days on the way home.
（然後我們就飛到墨西哥市，回家的途中在聖安東尼停了幾天。）

A What did you do in Mexico City?
（你在墨西哥市做什麼？）

B We were actually outside the city.
（實際上，我們在市區外。）

My husband's family has a vacation home there.
（我的夫家在那兒有一棟度假別墅。）

A It sounds great.
（聽起來太好了。）
You certainly look well rested.
（你看起來真的是充分休息了。）

句型靈活應用

· **只做了某事怎麼說？**

All I did was play and rest and have a ton of fun.
（我所做的就是玩、休息，和一大堆樂趣。）

All I did in the whole summer was sleep and eat.
（整個夏天我所做的就是吃和睡。）

文法句型練習

> You certainly look ＋形容詞
> （你看起來確實～）

＊ look 後面要接形容詞，本句中用過去分詞 "rested" 當形容詞，形容詞之前還有副詞 well 來修飾它。

▶ You certainly look well rested.
（你看起來真的是有充分的休息。）

談天必用單字

coast	[kost]	海岸（指沿海省份）

談天必用片語

a ton of		許多

Unit

MP3-62

I hear you are driving to Florida for your vacation.

（我聽說你打算開車去佛羅里達度假。）

談度假計劃

🅰 I hear you are driving to Florida for your vacation.

（我聽說你打算開車去佛羅里達度假。）

🅱 Yes, we're planning on two weeks.

（是的，我們打算度假兩星期。）

🅰 That should be fun.

（那應該很有趣。）

🅱 I think it will be.

（我想也是。）

We're going to take our time and stop when we feel like it.

（我們會一路慢慢走，愛停哪兒就停哪兒。）

We have reservations at Disney World for

Sunday through Tuesday.

（我們已經在迪斯奈樂園訂了從禮拜天到禮拜二的票。）

A You have lots of time to get there then.

（那你到那裏的時間很充裕。）

B Yes, we planned it so that we don't have to drive more than three or four hours a day.

（是的，我們計劃一天開車最多不超過三到四個小時。）

句型靈活應用

- **想用多久就用多久，怎麼說？**

There is no hurry. Please take your time.

（這事不急，你慢慢來。）

We're going to take our time and have a good look at it.

（我們要從從容容的，好好地看清楚。）

文法句型練習

> 子句＋ so that ＋子句
> 　（以致於～；以便～）

＊ so that 連接前後兩個子句，前面的子句是要做的事，後面的子句是目的。

▶ We planned it so that all the guests have a chance to talk.

（我們這樣計劃，以便所有的客人都有機會交談。）

▶ **Leave early so that you won't miss the bus.**
（早一點離開，以免你錯過巴士。）

reservation	[rɛzə'veʃən]	預訂
canoe	[kə'nu]	獨木舟
hurry	['hɝɪ]	趕時間
guest	[gɛst]	客人

take one's time		從容從事

Unit

62

MP3-63

We just got back from Italy.
（我們剛從義大利回來。）

談旅遊

🅐 Where have you been?
（你去哪裏了？）
I haven't seen you for a couple of weeks.
（我好幾禮拜沒看到你了。）

🅑 We just got back from Italy.
（我們剛從義大利回來。）

🅐 How fun!
（多有意思。）
Where did you go?
（你都去了什麼地方？）

🅑 We went to Rome, Naples, Florence, and of course over to the ruins of Pompeii.
（我們去了羅馬、那不勒斯、佛羅倫斯，當然也去了龐貝廢墟。）

🅐 What did you do?
（你在那兒做了什麼？）

B We toured a bunch of old cathedrals.

（我們看過很多老教堂。）

We took a trip to Venice and rode in the canal boats.

（我們也去了一趟威尼斯，在河道上坐船。）

And everywhere we went we ate and ate and ate.

（還有，不管我們到什麼地方，我們就是一直吃個不停。）

A Do you have any pictures?

（你有沒有拍什麼照片？）

I'd love to see them.

（我很想看看。）

B Sure, I should have them back sometime next week.

（當然，我下個禮拜可以把照片拿回來。）

句型靈活應用

· 要看照片，怎麼說？

Do you have any pictures?

（你有沒有拍照片呢？）

May I see your pictures?

（我可以看你的照片嗎？）

I'm going out of town on business sometime next week.

（下個禮拜我會有段時間去出差。）

I'm buying a computer sometime next year.

（明年我會找個時間買部電腦。）

> 主詞＋ have ＋過去分詞＋ for 一段時間
>   （這段時間內～）

＊ 當一個句子裏有指明一段時間（for 一段時間）時，時態用現在完成式，表示這段時間所做的事。

▶ **I haven't seen you for a couple of weeks.**
（好幾個星期沒有看到你了。）

▶ **I haven't watched TV for the last few days.**
（最近好幾天我都沒有看電視。）

▶ **I have known John for five years.**
（我認識約翰已經快五年了。）

談天必用單字

ruins	[ˈruɪnz]	廢墟
tour	[tʊr]	參觀
cathedral	[kəˈθidrəl]	教堂
ride	[raɪd]	坐
canal	[kəˈnæl]	運河
canal boat	[kənæl ˈbot]	運河上的船

談天必用片語

a bunch of		很多
take a trip to		到某地去旅行

Chapter 15

交易買賣

Unit

63

MP3-64

Looking around some.
（隨便看看。）

到車行看車

S How are you?
（你好嗎？）
Planning on buying a new car today?
（今天要買車嗎？）

C Looking around some.
（我隨便看看。）

S I've got a great deal on this sports car.
（這部跑車我可以給你一個好價錢。）
How about a test drive?
（要不要試開一下？）

C I'm not looking for a sports car.
（我不要看跑車。）

S What kind of car are you looking for?
（那你在看什麼車呢？）

C Something that has enough room for my family.
（大一點可以容納全家的車。）

S Well, I've got some great vans over here.
（是嗎，我那邊有幾部旅行小巴士。）

句型靈活應用

· **店員問你要買什麼，你怎麼回答？**

Looking around some.
（我隨便逛逛看。）

I'm just looking around.
（我只是逛逛而已。）

· **如何向顧客推銷產品？**

I've got a great deal on this sports car.
（這部跑車我可以很便宜賣給你。）

談天必用單字

sports car	['sports kɑr]	跑車
van	[væn]	旅行小巴士
room	[rum]	空間
test drive	['tɛst 'draɪv]	試開

談天必用片語

look for	尋找
what kind of	什麼樣子的

Unit

64

MP3-65

I'm looking for a new living room set.
（我在找一套新的客廳傢俱。）

買傢俱

C I'm looking for a new living room set.
（我在找一套客廳用的新傢俱。）

S We have a lot of very comfortable sets.
（我們這裏有很多套很舒服的傢俱。）
What style did you have in mind?
（你心裏有沒有特別喜歡的樣式？）

C It really doesn't matter.
（樣式不太要緊。）
I need something that is comfortable.
（我需要的是舒適。）

S Try this sofa out.
（那請試這一套沙發。）
And you won't find a better buy.
（價錢上你不會找到更便宜的了。）

C The color won't go with my carpet.
（可是這顏色和我的地毯不相配。）

S We can order it in any color you want.
（那我們可以幫你定你喜歡的顏色。）

· 告訴對方這是最好的交易了，怎麼說？

It's a good buy. （這個東西賣得很便宜。）

You won't find a better buy. （你不會找到比這個更便宜的了。）

文法句型練習

> It is one of ＋最高級形容詞＋名詞複數形
> （是最～其中一個）

＊ 本句型是形容詞最高級的用法之一，表示「最怎麼樣的其中一個」。
所以 one of 後面的最高級形容詞所修飾的名詞要用「複數形」。

▶ It is one of our most popular sofas.
（那是我們最受歡迎的沙發之一。）

▶ It is one of the most popular styles.
（那是最受歡迎的樣式之一。）

▶ He is one of the most talented students.
（他是最有天分的學生之一。）

談天必用單字

comfortable	['kʌmfɚtəbl̩]	舒適
popular	['pɑpjələ˞]	受歡迎
carpet	['kɑrpɪt]	地毯
order	['ɔrdɚ]	定貨

談天必用片語

| go with | 搭配 |
| try out | 試貨 |

Unit
65

I'm looking for a new computer.
（我在找一部新的電腦。）

在電腦店

C I need a new computer.
（我要買一部電腦。）

S Well, you've come to the right place.
（行，你來對地方了。）
We have the newest computers and accessories anywhere.
（我們這裏有最新的電腦和配備。）
What model did you have in mind?
（你心裏有沒有喜歡的機型？）

C I really don't know.
（我實在不清楚。）
As much as I can get in my price range.
（只能在我付得起的價錢範圍內盡量買好一點。）

S Come on over here and I'll show you the different models we have.
（請過來這邊，我讓你看我們這兒的不同機型。）
And then you can decide which you would prefer.
（然後你再決定你喜歡哪一種。）

· **問對方是否要買特定的東西，怎麼說？**

What model did you have in mind?
（你有沒有特別喜歡的機型？）

What style did you have in mind?
（你心裏有沒有特別喜歡的樣式？）

Did you have something particular in mind?
（你心裏有沒有特別想買什麼？）

文法句型練習

| 主詞＋動詞＋疑問子句 |

＊ which 所帶出的疑問子句做 decide 和 know 的受詞，表示「哪一個？」。

▶ I can't decided which I would prefer.
（我不能決定我到底要買什麼。）

▶ I know which I like best.
（我知道我最喜歡哪一個。）

談天必用單字

accessory	[əkˈsɛsərɪ]	配備
range	[rendʒ]	範圍
model	[ˈmɑdl̩]	機型
decide	[dɪˈsaɪd]	決定
prefer	[prɪˈfɝ]	比較喜歡
particular	[pɚˈtɪkjələ]	特別

談天必用片語

have something in mind	心裏有概念

I really need to think about it for a few days.

（我真的需要考慮幾天。）

在車行看車

S This is the perfect car for you.

（這部車對你最完美。）

It rides great, the a/c is cold, very roomy and comfortable.

（開起來最順手，冷氣夠冷，又寬敞又舒適。）

C I don't know.

（我不知道。）

I really need to think about it for a few days.

（我真的需要再考慮幾天。）

S Well, that's all right.

（是嘛，那沒有關係。）

But I can't guarantee we'll still have it.

（但我不能保證到時候車子還在。）

There are a couple of other folks looking at it.

（還有幾個其他的人在看。）

C If it isn't here, then it wasn't the car for me.

（要是車子賣掉了，那就注定那車子不是我的。）

I need to think about it.

（我需要考慮考慮。）

S What would it take to get you to drive this beauty home today?

（有什麼辦法讓你今天就把車子開回家呢？）

C Nothing.

（不用了。）

It is a big decision to buy a new car.

（買車是個大的決定。）

And I will not make a decision right now.

（我現在不願做決定。）

I am going to think about it for a few days.

（我需要幾天時間考慮。）

句型靈活應用

· **你不能決定要不要買，怎麼說？**

I need to think about it.

（我需要考慮。）

I am going to think about it for a few days.

（我要考慮幾天。）

it 當虛主詞

* 本句型是以 it 做「虛主詞」，真正的主詞是稍後的不定詞。例
如以下例句中的 to buy a new car 和 to drive this beauty home
today 才是句子的主題。

▶ It is a big decision to buy a new car.
（買車是個大的決定。）

▶ What would it take to get you to drive this
beauty home today?
（有什麼辦法能讓你今天就把車開回家呢？）

談天必用單字

a/c	[ˈeˈsi]	冷氣
roomy	[ˈrumɪ]	寬敞
beauty	[ˈbjutɪ]	美麗
decision	[dɪˈsɪʒən]	決定

談天必用片語

| make a decision | 做決定 |

Chapter 16

協議談判

Unit

67

MP3-68

I think the price is too high.

（我認為價錢太高了。）

買車時討價還價

A I think $5,000 is too high for a ten-year-old car.

（我認為一部十年的車 5,000 元實在太貴了。）

I will give $3,500 for it.

（我只出到 3,500 元。）

B This car is in superb condition.

（這部車子情況特別好。）

I'll let you have it for $4,500.

（我 4,500 元賣給你。）

A The body is in good condition.

（外觀看起來是很好。）

But it has a lot of miles on the engine, $4,000.

（但是引擎的里程數高了一點。4,000 元。）

B It has been maintained perfectly.

（這部車保養得非常好。）

I can't go below $4,500.
（4,500 元以下我不賣。）

A I can't go that high.

（我也不能出到那麼高。）

How about $4,250?
（4,250 元如何？）

B That sounds fair enough.

（聽起來還算公道。）

You have yourself a car.
（賣給你了。）

- **說某部車開過的哩程數很高，怎麼說？**

  The car has a lot of miles on the engine.

  （這部車的引擎哩程數很高。）

- **表示對方所提的還算合理，怎麼說？**

  That sounds fair enough.

  （聽起來還算公道。）

- **同意以對方出的價錢賣車給對方，怎麼說？**

  You have yourself a car.

  （車子賣給你了。）

文法句型練習

主詞＋ have(has) ＋ been ＋過去分詞
（已經被～）

* 本句型是「現在完成式被動語態」，時態上是「現在完成式」，語態是「被動式」。

▶ It has been maintained perfectly.
（它保養得很好。）

▶ The room looks nice. It has been cleaned.
（這個房間看起來很好，它已經清理過了。）

▶ I'm not going to the party. I haven't been invited.
（我不要去參加宴會，我沒有接到邀請。）

談天必用單字

superb	[sjuˈpɝb]	狀況很好
maintain	[menˈten]	保養
body	[bɑdɪ]	外觀
condition	[kənˈdɪʃən]	情況
engine	[ˈɛndʒən]	引擎
perfect	[ˈpɝfɪkt]	完美

談天必用片語

in good condition		情況很好

Unit

MP3-69

We can beat that price.

（我們可以賣得更便宜。）

講價錢和談條件

🅐 I have another supplier who will sell me the machine at $68.00.

（我有另外一個供應商，願意以 68 元賣我這種同型機器。）

🅑 We can beat that price.

（我們可以賣得更便宜。）

How about $67.80?

（67 元 8 角如何？）

🅐 Can you deliver within 48 hours of ordering?

（你能不能在定貨 48 小時內送貨？）

🅑 Not at that price.

（以這樣的價錢不行。）

I'd need four days.

（我需要四天。）

A I'd love to do business with you.

（我是很想和你做生意。）

But that won't cut it.

（但是不行也沒辦法。）

B What if I can get it to you within 72 hours?

（要是 72 小時給你送貨，如何？）

A That would be fine.

（那倒還可以。）

· **告訴對方這種條件你不能接受，怎麼說？**

That won't cut it.

（沒辦法就是沒辦法。）

· **告訴對方我們可以賣得更便宜，怎麼說？**

We can beat that price.

（我們可以勝過那個價錢。）

句型文法練習

who 當關係代名詞

* who 當「關係代名詞」，代替它前面的名詞並連結兩個句子。
例如以下例句中 who 分別指 playmate 和 supplier。

▶ I'm looking for a playmate who can play tennis very well.

（我正在找一位網球打得很好的球伴。）

▶ I have another supplier who will sell me the machine at $68.00.

（我另外有一個供應商願意賣給我同型機器，68 元一部。）

談天必用單字

supplier	[sə'plaɪr]	供應商
playmate	['plemet]	球伴

談天必用片語

what if	要是

Unit

69

We can reach some sort of agreement.

（我們可以達成一些協議。）

父母與兒女協定夜歸時間

A Let's see if we can reach some sort of agreement over your curfew.

（讓我們來看看，是不是能針對你的夜歸時間達成什麼協議。）

B Okay. Everyone else's parents let them stay out until two or three in the morning.

（好吧，別人的父母都讓他們玩到早上兩三點。）

A Well, I'm not everyone else's father.

（是嗎，可是我不是別人的爸爸。）

I think you need to be in the house by ten o'clock.

（我認為你十點鐘必須回到家。）

B That's absurd.

（那太荒謬了。）

I know junior high kids who can stay out later

than that.
（我知道初中的小孩都可以留得比那個時間晚。）

🄰 I'll be worried when you stay out late.

（如果你在外面待到太晚我會擔心。）

🄱 Okay, how about a midnight curfew?

（好吧，十二點如何？）

And I'll let you know where I am.
（更何況我會讓你知道我在什麼地方。）

🄰 That sounds quite reasonable.

（聽起來還算合理。）

句型靈活應用

・ **在某事達成協議，怎麼說？**

Let's see if we can reach some sort of agreement over your curfew.

（讓我們看看，對於你的夜歸時間是不是可以達成什麼協議。）

Let's see if we can reach an agreement over your TV-watching time.

（讓我們來看看，對於你看電視的時間是不是可以達成什麼協議。）

We can't reach an agreement over the price.

（我們在價錢上沒法達成什麼協議。）

・ **建議對方做某事，怎麼說？**

I think you need to take a computer course.

（我想你應該選一些電腦課。）

I think you need to go to bed early.

（我想你應該早一點去睡覺。）

文法句型練習

> 主詞＋動詞＋ if 子句
> （是否～）

＊ if 所帶出的子句做受詞用。

▶ Let's see if we can reach an agreement.

（讓我們來看看是不是能達成什麼協議。）

▶ The doctors aren't sure if he'll be all right.

（所有的醫生都不能確定他是不是能復原。）

談天必用單字

curfew	[ˈkɝfju]	戒嚴
reasonable	[ˈrizənəbl̩]	合理
absurd	[əbˈsɝd]	荒謬

談天必用片語

stay out late		逗留很晚

Chapter 17

發牢騷

Unit

70

MP3-71

I'm tired of it.

（我很厭煩了。）

買了新車，卻一直有毛病

A I bought this car two months ago.
（我兩個月前買了這部車。）
And it has been in the shop six times already.
（到現在已經進廠六次了。）

B We can't fix it unless we know about the problem.
（我們也得發現問題在哪裏，才能修呀。）

A I'm tired of it.
（我已經很厭煩了。）
I expect a new car to be new.
（我預期新車就是新車。）
I didn't have this many problems with my old car.
（就是我的老車也沒有這麼多毛病。）

B We are fixing the problems as soon as they happen.
（我們是隨時有毛病隨時修。）
That's the best we can do.
（我們能做的，最多也只是這樣了。）

A I need to speak to the General Manager.
（我要跟你的總經理談談。）

B Let me go find him for you.
（我去把他找來。）

句型靈活應用

- **表示你的厭煩，怎麼說？**

I'm tired of it.
（我很厭煩了。）

- **告訴對方你已盡了最大努力，怎麼說？**

That's the best we can do.
（我們最多只能做到這裏。）

- **去做某事，口語上用 go，後面直接加原形動詞**

Let me go find him for you.
（我去幫你把他找來。）

Go get a piece of paper for me.
（你去幫我找張紙來。）

文法句型練習

主詞＋過去式動詞＋過去的時間
主詞＋ have(has) ＋過去分詞＋ already

＊ 用「過去式」動詞是表示描述的事發生在過去的某個時候，而「現在完成式」have(has)＋過去分詞的形式只表示事情已經發生，但不特別指哪個時間。

▶ I bought this car two months ago.
（我兩個月前買了這部新車。）

▶ It has been in the shop six times already.
（到現在已經進廠六次。）

Unit

71

MP3-72

This traffic is awful.
（交通好亂。）

Ⓐ This traffic is awful.
（這種交通真是糟糕。）

Ⓑ It's not as bad as it was yesterday.
（今天沒有昨天那麼差。）
There was a wreck in the middle of the intersection then.
（昨天在十字路口中央就撞了車。）

Ⓐ People keep cutting in and out.
（大家一直切進切出。）
There's going to be one today.
（今天也一定要撞車。）

Ⓑ Just let them in so they don't hit you.
（就讓他們切進來好了，以免撞上你。）

Ⓐ This is ridiculous.
（這太過分了。）
I've got to find another way home.
（我看我必須找其他的路回家。）

句型靈活應用

· **抱怨交通狀況，怎麼說？**

This traffic is awful.

（這種交通實在糟糕。）

· **十字路口的中央，怎麼說？**

My car stopped in the middle of the intersection yesterday.

（我的車子昨天在十字路口的正中央熄火。）

文法句型練習

主詞＋現在式動詞＋ as ～ as ＋主詞＋過去式動詞

＊ 本句型是比較現在和過去的狀況。前面的子句是現在式，後面的子句是過去式，中間以「形容詞原級」的否定句連結起來，表示現在和過去不同了。

▶ It is not as bad as it was yesterday.

（今天沒有昨天的差。）

▶ She is not as pretty as she was before.

（她現在沒有以前那麼漂亮。）

談天必用單字

awful	[ˈɔfl̩]	很糟
intersection	[ˌɪntɚˈsɛkʃən]	十字路口
ridiculous	[rɪˈdɪkjələs]	可笑

Unit

72

MP3-73

This isn't what I ordered.
（這不是我點的。）

告訴服務生送錯菜了

A Excuse me, this isn't what I ordered.

（對不起，這不是我點的菜。）

B I'm sorry.

（對不起。）

Didn't you order shrimp fried rice?
（你不是點蝦仁炒飯嗎？）

A I ordered chicken fried rice.

（我點的是雞炒飯。）

B Oh, all I heard was shrimp fried rice.

（噢，我聽到的是蝦仁炒飯。）

Let me have the kitchen redo this for you.
（我讓廚房再做一道給你。）

A Thanks.

（謝謝了。）

B No problem. It will be a few minutes.
（沒問題，不過要等幾分鐘。）

句型靈活應用

· **不相符合，怎麼說？**

This isn't what I ordered.
（這不是我點的菜。）

This style isn't what I have in mind.
（這種樣式不是我所想的。）

· **請對方稍等一下，怎麼說？**

It will be a few minutes.
（那要等幾分鐘。）

文法句型練習

> Didn't you ＋原形動詞？
> （你不是～嗎？）

* 本句型是否定疑問句，問對方「你不是怎麼樣嗎？」

▶ Didn't you order shrimp fried rice?
（你不是點了蝦仁炒飯嗎？）

▶ Didn't you go to bed early last night?
（你昨天晚上不是很早就睡了嗎？）

> Let ＋ me ＋ have ＋受詞＋原形動詞
> 　（讓我叫某人做～）

＊ 本句型有兩個使役動詞 let 和 have。let me 後面用原形動詞
　have，不能用 has 或 had，而 have 之後的動詞也一定要用原形
　動詞。

▶ **Let me have the kitchen redo this for you.**
（我叫廚房再給你做一道。）

▶ **Let me have the secretary type a new one for you.**
（我叫秘書再打一份新的給你。）

談天必用單字

redo	[rɪˋdu]	再做一次
shrimp	[ʃrɪmp]	蝦
fried	[fraɪd]	炒
kitchen	[ˋkɪtʃən]	廚房

Unit
73

The picture is real fuzzy.
（畫面真的很模糊。）

向有線電視公司抱怨電視的畫面不好

🅐 Hello, I'm having a problem with my cable service.

（喂，我的有線電視有問題。）

🅑 What seems to be the problem?

（問題出在哪裏？）

🅐 The picture is real fuzzy.

（畫面很模糊。）

It won't come in clear at all.
（收進來的一點都不清晰。）

🅑 Are you sure it is the cable and not your TV?

（你確定是纜線而不是你的電視機嗎？）

🅐 Yes, I'm sure.

（是的，我很確定。）

🅑 All right then.

（那好吧。）

I will send a repairman there tomorrow.
（我明天派個修理員過去。）

句型靈活應用

· 如何提出抱怨？

I'm having a problem with my cable service.
（我的有線電視有問題。）

· 接到抱怨，如何回答？

What seems to be the problem?
（你的問題是什麼？）

· 問對方是否很肯定？

Are you sure it is the cable and not your TV?
（你確定那是你的纜線而不是你的電視嗎？）

Are you sure it is the wind and not someone knocking on the door?
（你確定那是風而不是有人在敲門嗎？）

談天必用單字

picture	['pɪktʃɚ]	畫面
fuzzy	['fʌzɪ]	模糊
repairman	[rɪ'pɛrmən]	修理工人
cable	['kebl̩]	纜線
service	['sɝvɪs]	服務

Unit

MP3-75

The expressway is a mess.
（高速公路真的一團糟。）

談高速公路塞車

🅐 Boy, is the expressway a mess?
（哇，高速公路這麼亂？）
With all the construction, it really slows traffic down.
（這些施工真的把車速弄慢下來了。）

🅑 It's not just the construction though.
（不僅僅是因為施工。）
Every day there are at least three or four major wrecks.
（每天都有三到四個重大車禍。）

🅐 I know. Did you see the one this morning?
（我知道，今天早上的那個你看到了嗎？）

🅑 Yes. I did.
（是的，我看到了。）

句型靈活應用

· 表示不只這一件事而已，怎麼說？

It's not just the construction though.
（不僅只是因為施工而已。）

237

It's not just the price though.
（不僅只是因為價錢而已。）

・ 說明由於甚麼的緣故，怎麼說？

With all the construction, it really slows traffic down.
（這些施工真的把交通弄慢下來了。）

With all your effort, you sure will succeed.
（盡你全力，你真的會成功。）

談天必用單字

expressway	[ɪksˈprɛswe]	高速公路
mess	[mɛs]	亂
construction	[kənsˈtrʌkʃən]	施工
traffic	[ˈtræfɪk]	交通
major	[ˈmedʒɚ]	主要
though	[ðo]	當然
wreck	[rɛk]	交通事故
involve	[ɪnˈvɑlv]	參與
effort	[ˈɛfɚt]	努力
succeed	[səkˈsid]	成功

談天必用片語

slow down	慢下來

Chapter 18

詢問資訊

Unit

75

MP3-76

Do you have any apartment available?
（你有空的公寓嗎？）

找公寓

A I'm looking for an apartment.
（我在找公寓。）

Do you have any available?
（你們這兒有沒有？）

B Yes, we do.
（有，我們有。）

Do you want a one or two-bedroom?
（你要一間臥室，還是兩間臥室？）

A A two-bedroom would be nice.
（兩間臥室比較好。）

But I don't know if I can afford it.
（但我不知道是不是付得起。）

B Our two-bedroom is $800 a month.
（我們兩間臥室的是一個月 800 元。）

But we have a one-bedroom with a study for only $725.

（不過，我們有一間臥室外加一間書房的，只要 725 元。）

A The one-bedroom with a study sounds nice.

（一間臥室外加一間書房，聽起來不錯。）

May I see it?

（我可以參觀嗎？）

B Of course, let me show it to you now.

（當然，我現在就帶你去看。）

句型靈活應用

- **問有沒有空的公寓，怎麼說？**

I'm looking for an apartment. Do you have any available?

（我想租公寓，你們這邊有沒有？）

Do you have any two-bedroom apartment available?

（你們這邊有沒有兩間臥室的公寓？）

Do you have a single room available?

（還有單人房的公寓嗎？）

- **徵求對方的同意，怎麼說？**

May I see it?

（我可以看看嗎？）

May I come in?
（我可以進來嗎？）

Let me show it to you.
（讓我把東西給你看看。）

I'll show you my stamp collection.
（讓我給你看我的集郵。）

文法句型練習

> I don't know if ～
>   （我不知道～是否～）

＊ if 所帶出來的子句做 I don't know 的受詞，指我所不知道的「事」。

▶ I don't know if I can afford it.
（我不知道是不是能付得起。）

▶ I don't know if the answer is right.
（我不知道答案對不對。）

two-bedroom apartment
（兩房的公寓）

＊ 兩房的公寓，「兩房」是一個單字形容詞，所以 two 和 bedroom 中間要有連結號 "-"，而 bedroom 也不可以用複數形。口語中語意很清楚時，名詞 apartment 可以省略。

▶ I'm looking for a two-bedroom apartment.

（我在找一間有兩間臥室的公寓。）

▶ A two-bedroom would be nice.
（兩間臥室的比較好。）

談天必用單字

afford	[əˈfɔrd]	付得起錢
available	[əˈveləbḷ]	還有空位
study	[ˈstʌdɪ]	書房

Unit

76

MP3-77

What positions are you hiring for?
（你們要請什麼職位的人？）

應徵工作前先詢問消息

Ⓐ Excuse me, I saw your sign saying "Help wanted".
（對不起，我看到你的招牌寫「雇用人員」。）

What positions are you hiring for?
（你們要雇用的是什麼樣的職位呢？）

Ⓑ You would need to speak with the manager.
（那你必須跟經理談。）

I can give you an application to fill out.
（我可以給你一張申請表讓你填。）

Ⓐ That would be great.
（那很好。）

But do you know what jobs are available?
（不過，你知道什麼樣的工作有缺嗎？）

Ⓑ We have openings in every department right

now.

（我們各部門現在都有空缺。）

Ⓐ Really, why do you have so many positions available?

（真的，你們為什麼會有那麼多空缺呢？）

Ⓑ We're in the middle of an expansion.

（因為我們正在擴張。）

And the corporate office keeps transferring people to other stores.

（而且總公司總是把人手調到別的店去。）

Ⓐ Thanks for your help.

（謝謝你的幫助。）

I'll get this application filled out now.

（我現在就把這張申請表填一填。）

句型靈活應用

· **告訴別人公司正在擴展，怎麼說？**

We're in the middle of an expansion.

（我們正在擴展當中。）

文法句型練習

> 主詞＋ see（saw）＋受詞＋現在分詞

＊ 感官動詞 see 後面可加「原形動詞」或「現在分詞」，用現在分詞表示你看到的那件事「正在進行著」。

▶ I saw your sign saying "Help wanted".
（我看到你的招牌寫「雇用人員」。）

▶ I saw the children playing outside.
（我看到小孩在外面玩。）

get ＋受詞＋過去分詞

＊ get 是「使役動詞」，使役動詞如果以「事物」當受詞時，因為事物自己不會做動作，所以接下去的動詞要用過去分詞，表示被動。

▶ I'll get this application filled out.
（我會把這張申請表填一填。）

▶ When can you get it done?
（你幾時會做好？）

談天必用單字

application	[ˌæplɪˈkeʃən]	申請表
position	[pəˈzɪʃən]	職位
available	[əˈveləbḷ]	有缺
corporate	[ˈkɔrpəret]	公司
transfer	[ˈtrænsfɚ]	調差

談天必用片語

fill out	填表

Unit

MP3-78

Could you tell me where the courthouse is?
（你可否告訴我法院在哪裏？）

問路

A Excuse me, could you tell me where the courthouse is?

（對不起，你能告訴我法院在什麼地方嗎？）

B Which courthouse do you want?

（你指的是哪一個法院？）

A Oh, I forget there's more than one.

（噢，我忘了法院不只一個。）

I need the County courthouse.
（我要問的是縣法院。）

B No problem.

（沒有問題。）

Just go straight down Elm Street and it is on your left.
（你往埃姆街直走下去，它就在你左邊。）

🅐 Thanks for your help.
（謝謝你的幫助。）

・**要問路，怎麼問？**

Could you tell me where the courthouse is?
（你能告訴我法院在哪裏嗎？）

Could you show me the way to the National bank?
（你能不能告訴我去國家銀行怎麼走？）

・**當你樂意幫對方忙時，怎麼說？**

No problem.
（沒有問題。）

courthouse	[ˈkortˌhaʊs]	法院
straight	[stret]	直接

Unit

78

May I help you?
（有什麼事嗎？）

在飛機場找不到行李

🅐 May I help you?

（可以為你效勞嗎？）

🅑 Yes, my baggage didn't come off the plane with every one else's.

（是的，我的行李沒有和其他人的行李一道下飛機。）

I guess I need to file a lost baggage claim.

（我想我需要填一份行李報失單。）

🅐 Not necessarily.

（不用了。）

What flight were you on?

（你搭的是幾次班機？）

🅑 Flight 457 from Chicago.

（457 次，從芝加哥來的。）

249

A Okay.
（好的。）

Some of the baggage for that flight was placed on flight 475 to Houston.
（那個班次的一些行李被放到 475 次飛休斯頓的班機上去了。）

However, we have already received it back here.
（不過，我們已經把它接回來了。）

Do you have your claim tickets?
（你有沒有行李單？）

B Yes, here they are.
（有，就在這裏。）

A I'll be right back with your luggage.
（我馬上把你的行李找出來給你。）

句型靈活應用

· 問對方有什麼事，怎麼說？

May I help you?
（有事可以為你效勞嗎？）

· 把對方要的東西給對方時，怎麼說？

Here they are.
（他們在這裏。）

文法句型練習

baggage 是不可數名詞

＊ 行李用 baggage 和 luggage 都可以，但要注意這兩個字都是「不可數」名詞，不能加 s。

▶ On a long trip, you need several pieces of baggage to carry your clothes in.
（長途旅行的時候，你需要好幾件行李來裝你的衣物。）

主詞＋ was ＋過去分詞
（某件東西被～）

＊ 本句型是「過去式的被動」，表示過去發生的事，但這件事是被動的。

▶ Some of the baggage for that flight was placed on flight 475 to Houston.
（該班次的一些行李被放到 475 次飛休斯頓的班機上了。）

▶ The books were placed on the book shelf.
（書本都被放回書架上去了。）

談天必用單字

file	[faɪl]	建檔
claim	[klem]	申領
baggage	[ˈbægɪdʒ]	行李
luggage	[ˈlʌgɪdʒ]	行李
flight	[flaɪt]	飛行班次

談天必用片語

come off		下飛機

一點靈！用眼睛學英語

英語系列：45

作者／張瑪麗
出版者／哈福企業有限公司
地址／新北市板橋區五權街16號
電話／(02) 2945-6285　傳真／(02) 2945-6986
郵政劃撥／31598840　戶名／哈福企業有限公司
出版日期／2018年1月
定價／NT$ 299元 (附MP3)

全球華文國際市場總代理／采舍國際有限公司
地址／新北市中和區中山路2段366巷10號3樓
電話／(02) 8245-8786　傳真／(02) 8245-8718
網址／www.silkbook.com 新絲路華文網

香港澳門總經銷／和平圖書有限公司
地址／香港柴灣嘉業街12號百樂門大廈17樓
電話／(852) 2804-6687　傳真／(852) 2804-6409
定價／港幣100元 (附MP3)

圖片／shuttlestock
email／haanet68@Gmail.com
網址／Haa-net.com
facebook／Haa-net 哈福網路商城

國家圖書館出版品預行編目資料

一點靈! 用眼睛學英語 / 張瑪麗著. -- 新
北市 : 哈福企業, 2018.01
　　面；　公分. -- (英語系列 ; 45)
ISBN 978-986-94966-7-4(平裝附光碟片)
1.英語 2.詞彙 3.會話

805.12　　　　　　　106025007